RIVALS

HARPER

An Imprint of HarperCollins*Publishers*

ALS

A BASEBALL GREAT NOVEL

TIM GREEN

ALSO BY TIM GREEN

BASEBALL GREAT NOVELS

Baseball Great
Rivals
Best of the Best

FOOTBALL GENIUS NOVELS

Football Genius
Football Hero
Football Champ
The Big Time

Rivals

Copyright © 2010 by Tim Green

Library of Congress Cataloging-in-Publication Data is available.
ISBN 978-0-06-162692-0 (trade bdg.) — ISBN 978-0-06-162693-7 (lib. bdg.)

Typography by Joel Tippie

10 11 12 13 14   CG/RRDH   10 9 8 7 6 5 4 3 2 1

❖

First Edition

For my boys, Thane, Troy, and Ty

CHAPTER ONE

WHEN THE SUN CAME blasting in through the hotel room curtains on Sunday morning, Josh pulled aside the shades and felt the thrill of being in a championship game wash over him like the sunlight. The feeling quickly sank into a sea of doubt. Being considered a great player by the Titans was one thing, but the better their team did, the better the competition became. There were other kids out there—not many, but they were there—whose skills rivaled Josh's. Josh's father— a mountain of a man who'd been a first-round draft pick out of high school but spent all of his thirteen years as a pro in the minor leagues—told Josh that if he wanted to be truly great, he had to relish the thought of a rivalry.

"Great players always want to go up against the

best," his father would say, "even if they don't win. A real rivalry is when teams or players go back and forth between who wins and loses so when they play each other, both are at their very best."

It bothered Josh that he didn't relish the thought of a good rivalry. He just couldn't help wishing for the kind of games where they swamped the other team. That's how it had been in this qualifying tournament so far, but Josh knew that it wouldn't be true today. He'd be up against the tournament's best pitcher, and the sickening dread smothering the thrill made him feel that he was something less than what his father wanted him to be.

These were the kind of feelings he could only talk about with one person—Jaden Neidermeyer. Somehow, her being a girl let him speak freely, and her perky reply hadn't made him sorry.

"Everything you do, Josh," she had said, "you do well. You work to be the best. If having a rival you look forward to is part of what it takes to be great, don't worry, it'll happen. Just be you, Josh. That's all you have to do."

Benji, his other best friend and roommate on the road, rolled over in his twisted pile of sheets and groaned.

"Turn it off," Benji said, blindly swatting the air.

"Come on," Josh said. "The Toledo Nighthawks are the only thing between us and the Hall of Fame Tournament in Cooperstown."

"Hall of Fame Tournament?" Benji asked, scrunching up his face.

"It's supposed to become the biggest thing in youth baseball!" Josh said. "It's the first major tournament of the summer. My dad said that this year they're going to have more people watching on TV than the Little League World Series. He said the teams are going to be the best of the best."

"You don't have to tell me how big it is; I'm a Cooperstown veteran," Benji said, pulling a pillow over his head that muffled his words. "You've seen my Babe Ruth paperweight, haven't you? The one where he's in a Red Sox uniform? That's how I like to think of him, the Red Sox being the greatest franchise in baseball history and all."

"But you never *played* there," Josh said, yanking Benji's covers off the bed. His oversized friend was wearing white boxer shorts spotted with red hearts.

Josh laughed, thankful for something to lighten his mood. "No wonder you wanted to undress in the dark. Where'd you get those things?"

"I can't help it if I'm a ladykiller," Benji said, his face turning as red as the hearts. He slipped sideways into the bathroom, covering as much of his shorts as he could.

"Ladykiller?" Josh said.

"Girls love a man with good taste in underwear," Benji said from behind the bathroom door.

"What are you talking about?" Josh said, still laughing. "No one's going to see your underwear—not any ladies, anyway—unless you're planning on flashing someone at the pool."

"It's not about what they see," Benji said, bursting forth from the bathroom with his baseball pants hiding the hearts. "It's an *attitude*. Women can smell it on you."

Josh could only shake his head as he ran a comb through his hair.

"Look at you," Benji said. "I know you're working yourself over in that mirror pretty hard for Jaden."

Josh rolled his eyes. "Cut it out. I didn't mean to hurt your feelings."

"Everyone knows she's crazy about you," Benji said, pulling on the rest of his uniform and pitching his voice like a girl's. *"Oh Josh, you're so strong. Is it even a challenge for you to hit a home run with those two-hundred-foot fences after playing all those games in U14?"*

Benji made kissing noises.

"Would you rather I *didn't* smack them over the fence?" Josh asked.

What Benji heard Jaden say was true. Until Josh and Jaden exposed his former coach, Rocky Valentine, for steroid dealing, Josh had been part of a U14 travel team. He'd gotten experience playing with kids two years older than he was on a field that was much bigger. The fence for U14 was at about three hundred feet instead of the two hundred feet for Little League, or U12. The bases, too, went down from ninety feet apart at U14 to sixty for U12. It was Josh's incredible vision—being able to see the ball the instant it left the pitcher's hand and read its spin—as well as his unusual size and strength for a twelve-year-old that let him keep up with the older kids.

With the strength-training program he'd been on with his old team—even though Josh never did use his old coach's steroids—he'd been able to hit home runs over the three-hundred-foot fence, so, more times than not, when Josh got all of the ball against a U12 pitcher, he put it out of the park. Josh's dad had kept the strength-training regimen as part of his own U12 team's preparation, only without the steroids. Along with Josh's incredible scoring ability, it had a lot to do with the Titans being so successful.

"Honestly?" Benji said, his eyebrows disappearing up underneath his dark bangs. "It gets a little disgusting."

"You like winning, though," Josh said with a grin as he pulled on his uniform.

"Everyone likes winning," Benji said. "Don't change the subject. Jaden is crazy for you, man, riding out here with the team, staying at our hotel. I know she's supposedly writing for the paper, but I think there's a lot more than Pulitzer Prizes on her mind. She probably has your name tattooed on her butt."

"Stop it. She's a nice girl, she loves baseball, and you know it. And I'm not the one with the hearts on my underwear," Josh said, zipping up his overnight bag and heading for the door. "I'll leave the girl stuff to you. I got baseball games to play. Come on. We'll be late for breakfast."

They took the elevator down and, to Josh's embarrassment, the first thing they saw when they walked into the restaurant was Jaden, a tall, pretty girl with honey-colored skin, green eyes flecked with yellow, and frizzy hair that she kept pulled back tight off her face. She sat at a round booth just inside the hostess stand calling Josh's name and waving frantically for them to come and sit down. Josh looked around and hung his head before slipping into the booth. Jaden was as good a friend to him as Benji, and he wasn't going to stop being nice to her just because he hated Benji's teasing.

"Sit down," Jaden said. "Listen to this! I was checking out this Toledo team, and you guys can't believe what I heard."

"They've got Sandy Planczeck, the best pitcher in the state of Ohio," Benji said, yawning and picking up his menu. "He throws a seventy-five-mile-an-hour fastball. Yeah, yeah, yeah, we know. Josh could barely get to sleep last night. How's the pancakes in this joint?"

Jaden scowled at Benji and said, "He throws a

seventy-five-mile-an-hour fastball, yes, but it's what he's planning on doing with it."

"Yeah," Benji said from behind the menu, "he's gonna strike out Josh. Oooh, now we're all scared. Josh'll knock it into the river."

In the park where they would play, beyond the fence was a road, and if the ball went another hundred feet or so past that, it would hit the Genesee River.

"No, he's not going to try to strike out Josh, you goofball," Jaden said, pulling Benji's menu down. "If the Nighthawks need it to win, he's going to throw a beanball at Josh."

"You're kidding," Josh said, setting down his water glass without taking a drink.

"No," Jaden said, "I'm not. I was scouting them out in the semifinals yesterday, and I met his girlfriend."

"Planczeck's got a *girl*friend?" Josh said.

Jaden nodded. "She didn't know who I was and started bragging about him. I said I'd seen the Syracuse Titans, and they had a really great player named Josh LeBlanc who was almost six feet tall. That's when she told me they already knew about you and that if he needed to use it, her boyfriend had a surprise for you. She said it exactly, a beanball."

"*Bean*ball? What is that?" Benji asked, crinkling his face. "Like he farts in the middle of his windup?"

Jaden rolled her eyes. "You are so lame. A *beanball*. This guy's a headhunter."

Josh turned to Benji. "She means he's going to try and hit me with that seventy-five-mile-an-hour fastball.

"Right in the head."

CHAPTER TWO

"HE CAN'T DO THAT," Benji said, slapping his hand on the table so that the silverware jangled and the ice in their water glasses danced.

"Not legally," Jaden said. "But how do you prove it? It's up to the umpire's discretion to call it. If the ump just says it's a wild pitch, there's not much you can do. The Nighthawks probably know that if Josh stays on pace and they want to win, they'll have to get him out of the game."

"We've got to tell your dad," Benji said to Josh.

Josh shook his head. "And look like I'm scared of some kid's fastball? I know just what my dad's going to say to that. 'Step up to the plate and act like a man.' That's my dad."

"Not if he knew the guy was going to try to hurt

you," Jaden said. "Your dad's tough, but he's not ice-cold."

Josh held up his hand, signaling them to stop. "I'm *not* saying anything to my dad. Now I know it's coming, I can just keep an eye out and duck if he throws for my head."

Benji whistled low and raised his menu again. "I don't know. Seventy-five miles an hour."

The waitress arrived. They had breakfast and joined the rest of the team milling toward the bus. Coach Moose, a thick-necked middle school gym teacher who worked as his father's assistant, stopped Josh before he got on and said, "Josh, will you go tell your dad I got everyone here. I told him nine, but the bus driver says there's some parade we've got to go around, and it'll take us longer than we thought."

"Sure," Josh said. He headed through the lobby and up the elevator to the room where his mom and dad were staying with his baby sister, Laurel.

As he turned the corner, he stopped at the sound of his parents arguing inside the room. A suitcase held the door open. In the background, his little sister babbled to herself. Josh backed against the wall, out of sight, and listened.

"Stop saying 'It's only a game,'" Josh's father said.

"How is it more than that, Gary?" his mother said. "How? You keep talking about Nike, but you've got a contract with them and you're doing fine."

Josh knew his dad's feelings about the Nike contract were as delicate as they were special. Coach Valentine lost the U14 Titans' sponsorship after the steroid scandal. Josh had heard jealous whispers about his father having had something to do with the steroids as well— a complete lie—and even that he orchestrated the old coach's demise so that he could grab the esteemed and valuable Nike deal.

"Because 'fine' doesn't mean anything," his father said. "Everyone's cutting back—Nike, too—and if they do, who knows what happens to the Titans? But if we win today, we qualify for the Hall of Fame National Championship Tournament. It's the biggest thing in Little League Baseball these days, and whoever wins *that* gets a guaranteed five-year deal. *That's* security, Laura, something I never had as a player. Something I want. Look at the house we live in. Drafts coming through the walls all winter. Plumbing going bad every other week. A doggone leak in the roof! I'd like to get us into something better before the place falls in on us, so stop saying it's only a game. It's not. This is our life we're talking about here."

"I just don't want Josh to feel that kind of pressure," his mom said, her voice softening.

"And I'd never do that," his father said, quieter now too. "And he won't. I'm not saying anything to him about it and I know you won't, so we're fine. To him, it *is* only a game."

Josh listened for a minute, thinking about his father's words and how he wished he hadn't heard them at all. Knowing how much was at stake made the sinking feeling of dread even worse. His mother muttered something he couldn't hear and his father answered in the same quiet tone before Josh heard him moving toward the door.

Josh backed up and then started walking again as though he'd just arrived.

"Hey Dad," he said, meeting him in the doorway and trying to read his mom's face from the corner of his eye. "Coach Moose says the bus has to leave now, something about a parade."

"Okay, grab that suitcase for your mom, will you, Josh?"

Josh did, and they loaded up his mom and sister before he and his dad stepped up onto the bus.

Jaden sat across the aisle from him, and after they were under way she leaned over and asked, "What's the matter?"

"Nothing," Josh said. "We have to win this thing, that's all."

"I don't know if you should put that kind of pressure on yourself, Josh," Jaden said.

"Why not?"

"Well," Jaden said, tapping her pen against the cover of her notepad, "I just think you play better when you're relaxed. Just go out there and play."

"I play the same no matter what," Josh said, angry because he knew it wasn't true.

"Okay," she said, "all I'm saying is that if you don't win this, it isn't going to ruin your life or anything."

Josh looked at her for a moment, then said, "That's where you're wrong."

CHAPTER THREE

GRAY COTTON CANDY CLOUDS hung from the sky, but the forecast didn't call for any rain and the temperature was in the low seventies. The Titans took the field for warm-ups and Josh studied the Nighthawks players in their dugout, wondering which one was Planczeck. He looked over at Jaden, who sat in the deep corner of their dugout with her notepad out, and gave her a questioning look. She just shrugged and shook her head. When an easy grounder came his way, Josh fumbled it and had to reach between his legs to get a hold before throwing wild to first. The first baseman missed it, and the ball hit the fence beyond the foul line.

"LeBlanc!" his father barked from the fence by the batter's circle. "Come on now, get your head into it!"

Josh winced and focused on the balls Coach Moose

peppered at them from behind the plate. The stands began to fill with parents, supporters, and just baseball fans who wanted to see what two of the top U12 Little League travel teams in the country looked like.

After "The Star-Spangled Banner," the Nighthawks took the field. Even after a short, stocky boy built like a fireplug headed for the mound chomping on a fat wad of bubble gum, Josh searched the Nighthawks dugout for the pitcher named Sandy Planczeck.

When the boy stepped up and began throwing warm-up pitches, Josh looked at Coach Moose, thinking about the prospect of a beanball, and asked, "Is *that* Planczeck?"

Moose glanced at him and said, "Yeah, you heard about his fastball?"

Josh swallowed at the sound of the ball smacking the catcher's mitt like a gunshot. The ball was a blur.

"I heard some things," Josh said, picking out the batting helmet he liked best and stepping aside for the three batters in front of him. Josh couldn't take his eyes off Planczeck's face, unable to decipher the pitcher's blank expression beneath the thatch of dirty blond hair poking out from under his red cap as his jaw worked steadily at the gum.

Since he batted cleanup, Josh never got the chance to swing. Planczeck put the top of the lineup down with just fourteen pitches, using a short, spring-loaded windup that somehow resulted in a fastball rarely seen at the U12 level. The Titans took their turn in the field. Their own top pitcher, Kerry Eschelman, gave up two hits but got out of the inning without a run after Josh scooped up a burner and the Titans made a double play.

His first time, Josh felt sweat greasing the bat handle beneath his grip. The first pitch came right down the middle and Josh didn't even get to swing.

"Strike!"

The second pitch came. Josh read it the instant it left Planczeck's hand: a ball—high, fast, and way inside. Josh fell back from the plate to avoid being hit but stumbled and went down on his butt. His helmet skittered across the dirt and his face went on fire with embarrassment when someone in the stands laughed out loud. From the dugout, Josh's father shook his head.

Josh got to his feet and stepped into the box. The third pitch came—nothing but heat down the middle, which confused Josh since he expected another potential beanball.

"Strike two!"

"Come on, Josh! You can hit this guy!" Josh's father yelled. "Swing! Don't just watch it!"

Josh stepped out of the box and wedged his helmet down tight. If Planczeck was going to try to bean him, there was nothing Josh could do. He'd have to hope his vision could get him out of the way quickly enough. He gritted his teeth and stepped in, ignoring Planczeck's blank stare and focusing instead on his hand and seeing the ball as it left the pitcher's fingertips. Curve, too far outside to be a strike. He let it go.

"Ball."

Josh stepped away from the 2–2 count, swung a couple times, then got back into the box, focusing on Planczeck's release. Another fastball.

Josh saw the line, a little high and a little outside, but still a strike.

He felt the grin infecting his face and swung big.

CHAPTER FOUR

THE BAT CRACKED AND the ball took off, clearing the fence by a mile, bouncing off the road beyond the field and rolling down the grassy bank on its way to the Genesee River below. The Titans fans and bench erupted.

Josh jogged around the bases, relieved, but unable to get Jaden's warning and the inside pitch out of his mind, and unable to keep from meeting Planczeck's eyes as he crossed the plate under the gaze of the pitcher's gum-chomping blank stare.

Esch began to wear down, but—led by Josh—the Titans played great defense and kept the score close enough so that by the beginning of the sixth, it was tied at four, with Josh having hit three home runs. While the Titans had to switch to another pitcher, Planczeck never seemed to fade. If Jaden *was* right and Planczeck really did plan to do what his girlfriend claimed, then now would be the time for a beanball. But, beanball or no beanball, Josh prayed he'd get another chance at bat. Anything to get them to the big Hall of Fame Tournament. But for him to even get the chance, they had to finish out their order with Benji, and then the first three batters before Josh. Somehow, two of the four would have to get on base.

Benji made the sign of the cross and stepped up to the plate. The first pitch came right at him, nailing him in the leg and dropping Benji like a sack of potatoes. Moose ran out and helped Benji to his feet. He limped down the line to first base, waving dramatically to the clapping crowd, his face a mask of agony. The next two batters struck out quick, but each one got an errant pitch that left Josh feeling certain that Planczeck was setting the stage for a beanball, getting the ump used to an occasional wild pitch to make it look unintentional. When Esch stepped up to the plate, everyone, including Esch, was surprised when he actually hit the ball, driving it through the opening between first and second.

Josh clapped and tightened his batting glove down before starting for the plate with two runners on base and two outs.

"Hang on," Josh's father said, gripping his shoulder and nodding toward the Nighthawks' dugout.

The Nighthawks coach had gone out to the mound. The coach talked with Planczeck before glancing over at Josh, whispering one more thing and then returning to his bench.

"They're going to walk you intentionally," Josh's father said, making a face. "The coach is calling for a ball. Nothing we can do about it."

"That's garbage," Josh said. If Planczeck gave him the opportunity, Josh could put the game out of reach, driving in two runs as well as scoring himself and giving the Titans a lead the Nighthawks couldn't likely recover from.

"You with three home runs already?" his father said, raising his eyebrows. "I can't say I wouldn't do it if I were them."

"Can I chase it?" Josh asked, imagining himself jumping forward and reaching for a really wide outside pitch.

His dad clamped his lips shut, then said, "You know what? Do that. Make him throw that sucker so far outside the catcher can't get it. I'll give the sign for Benji and Esch to steal."

Josh grinned and stepped up to the plate. He'd never seen anyone jump out at an intentional ball, but he'd heard of it happening, and if it could be done by anyone, he knew it was him. He stepped up and shared his grin with Planczeck, ready to go and concentrating hard on the pitcher's hand.

In the instant before the release of the ball, Josh sensed something wrong. As it left Planczeck's hand,

Jaden's words blasted fresh through his mind, mixing with disbelief. He'd been thinking fastball, high, but the laces told him curve. Josh hesitated for a fraction of a second, and it was too long. The pitch struck him in the face. Josh saw stars and felt his body spin for just a split second before everything went fuzzy.

CHAPTER FIVE

JOSH SMELLED GRASS AND hot dogs and he thought about eating one. Someone shook him.

"Josh! Josh! Everyone get back!"

Josh blinked and saw his dad blocking out the sky.

"Are you okay, Son? Do you hear me?"

Josh nodded slowly, the pain in his face and head making him wince. He didn't want to talk. He heard Jaden's voice laced with panic, telling people to get out of her way, and then her face appeared beside his father's. Something tickled Josh's upper lip and he wiped it and came away with a bright smear of blood.

"Oh my," Jaden said.

Josh saw the questioning look on his father's face. It was a look Josh wanted to obliterate. It wasn't a look of disgust or shame but of wonder, maybe even doubt about just what kind of a man Josh would become. Josh had heard the story several times from his father's teammates about him taking a novocaine shot directly into his shoulder joint so he could pitch in a double-A championship game.

Josh struggled upright and tried to stand.

"Whoa," Coach Moose said, gripping his arm.

Josh pushed him away and said, "I'm fine."

"You're bleeding," Jaden said.

"It's just a bloody nose," Josh said, even though it felt like a knife was sticking into the back of his eyeball.

He reached for his bat. "I'm fine."

"Okay," the ump said, "take your base."

Jaden pointed at Planczeck and shouted, "He did it on purpose! That was a beanball! His girlfriend told me about it yesterday. She's right over there."

"Take his base and that guy's out of the game," Josh's father said, pointing at Planczeck.

The umpire was a short, chubby man with a round, red face. He frowned from behind his mask, shrugged, and said, "A wild pitch, Coach."

"That's the second man he's hit in four batters, and it was intentional," Josh's dad said. "She said it."

"She? Who's *she*?" the ump said, casting Jaden a nasty look. "Pitchers don't get sat down unless they hit three batters, Coach."

"That's if he's not *trying* to hit them," his dad said. "That's your call. Use your judgment."

"I am using my judgment, Coach," the ump said. "And if you don't get out of my face, I'm tossing you out of the park."

"That's *terrible*," Jaden said.

"That's it," the ump said, stabbing the air with his thumb. "You're out of here, young lady."

"She's a reporter," Josh's dad said.

"I don't care who she is," the ump said. "Out of the park. If you don't leave, I'm stopping the game."

Jaden's face went pale and she turned to go.

"What about you, Coach?" the ump asked, adjusting the metal cage of his mask.

Josh's dad's face turned purple and he clenched his meaty fists. The ump swallowed and stepped back, but Josh's dad just turned and stamped away.

"Let's go," the ump said with a growl. "Clear the field. Take your base. Play ball. Son, I said, 'Take your base.'"

Josh stood holding his bat. Blood drizzled down the back of his throat, but he swallowed it so no one would know. "I don't have to, do I?"

"It's a free base," the ump said.

"I can still hit, though, can't I?"

Josh's father spun around and came back.

"Coach, you want him to advance, right?" the ump said.

"Josh," his father said, taking Josh's shoulders gently in his big hands. "Your eye is almost swollen shut. You've got a whopper. You should take the base."

Josh felt tears welling up in his good eye. His father

was giving him an easy way out. The smaller part of him wanted to take the base. They'd lose, and the toughest tournament in the country would pass them by. No Cooperstown—Josh and the Titans could spend the rest of the summer romping over lesser opponents. No pressure. No lead in his gut, weighing him down. Only sunshine and grand-slam home runs.

It felt like someone had driven a tent stake through his cheek, but he shook his head. "If I don't hit this, we're not going to win, Dad. I need to knock it out of here. I don't, and we don't get to Cooperstown. The best of the best. I heard you say it."

Josh's dad glanced up into the stands in the direction of his mom, then he bit into his lower lip, turned to the ump, and said, "Okay. Let him hit."

"Coach, it's—"

"He's *entitled* to advance to first," Josh's father said. "He doesn't *have* to. I know the rules. Section 6.08 (b). Why don't you read it?"

Obviously flustered, the umpire pulled the rule book out of his back pocket and began to flip through the pages.

"What's going on?" the Nighthawks coach asked, emerging from his dugout.

Josh's dad wheeled on him with clenched fists and a furious look on his face. "Josh isn't taking the base. He's entitled to it but not compelled. Even though your pitcher tried to knock him out of the game with your dirty tricks."

"Hey, easy, Coach, it was a wild pitch," the other coach said.

"Don't 'easy' me," Josh's dad growled, looming over the much smaller man. "I won't even say what ought to happen to you, but know this: Your pitcher has already hit two batters, and if he hits another, he's finished. So you just tell him to throw it in there and see if he can strike my kid out."

"He's right," the ump said, showing the other coach the rule book.

"Maybe play some baseball, Coach," Josh's father said as he stalked away, "and let's see who wins."

The ump shrugged. Josh wiped his good eye and stepped up to the other side of the plate, switching to lefty since he could only see now out of his right eye. Everyone cleared the infield and Planczeck stared at Josh with the same empty look and the same mindless chomping on his gum. This time he nodded, though, then went into his windup and fired a burner right down the middle.

Josh saw it coming, saw the seams, saw their spin, saw the path it would take, and knew just how to swing.

When the bat cracked, Josh gasped in pain.

CHAPTER SIX

JOSH'S BRAIN LIT UP with a Christmas display of pain, and even though the ball went out of the park, he staggered and needed to catch his breath as he ran down the first-base line. Jogging around the field, even the screams of the Titans fans and his teammates made him wince. When the Titans tried to swarm him in the dugout, he pushed them away.

"I can't," he said, shrinking from their backslaps. "Don't. I'm hurt."

"Josh?" his father said.

"It's okay, Dad," he said, catching himself on the bench and taking a seat, knowing the game wasn't over yet. "I just need some space."

The next batter went down on three pitches and it was the Titans' turn to take the field. They had a 7–4 lead, but now they had to protect it.

"Don't get excited yet," Josh's dad said in a growl to the team after calling them in to a huddle. "We need to play defense. They've scored the last two innings and they're at the top of their lineup, so this thing is far from over. Let's go, 'Believe' on three. One, two, three—"

"BELIEVE!"

Josh's dad took him by the arm and said, "You proved how tough you are, Josh. Let me put Lido at short and put a sub in for him in right field. That eye looks worse by the minute."

"I'm good, Dad," Josh said, trying to smile but unable to because of the pain. "We need this and, no offense to Benji, he's got a great glove, but he can't make the throw to first as good as me. I can play with this."

His dad bit into his lower lip, but he nodded and patted Josh on the back. As he headed out, he said, "That's why you got two of them, right?"

"Two of what?" Josh asked.

"Two eyes," his dad said. "In case one closes up, you got the other."

Josh smiled.

The Titans relief pitcher struggled mightily, walking two batters and giving up a double and two singles. It wasn't long before the Nighthawks had two more runs and the bases were loaded. Josh looked at the 7–6 score and felt sick, in part because of how much his face hurt, but mostly because it looked like the whole effort was for nothing.

Planczeck stepped up to the plate. One of the runs from earlier in the game was a homer by Planczeck, and Josh knew he'd be licking his chops for a chance to smash another one with the Titans pitcher struggling like he was. Planczek slapped the chalk on his glove and rubbed it with his other hand as he approached the box with the bat under his arm. Before he stepped to the plate, Planczeck looked right at Josh, offered up a tiny smirk, and pointed his bat at the fence like he was Babe Ruth.

Josh crouched down and smacked his hand into his glove, angling his head so his good eye could take in more of the action. On the first pitch, Planczeck swung so hard, he spun himself around.

"Strike one!" the ump called.

Planczeck seemed unfazed. He let the second pitch go by.

"Ball."

The third pitch was a ball as well. A 2–1 count. Planczeck wiggled his hips and cleats as though he was planting himself permanently into the dirt of the batter's box.

The next pitch came. Planczeck swung big and smacked it. Josh watched the ball leave the bat and he started to run. Planczeck had connected, but a bit more under the ball than what would carry it out of the park.

It floated for a moment, then started to plummet for the no-man's-land between the third baseman and the left fielder. Josh poured on his speed, calling off both his teammates.

He leaped for the ball, diving and reaching and praying he could make a miraculous catch.

CHAPTER SEVEN

JOSH HIT THE GROUND and saw red and orange lightning bolts of pain. He felt himself drifting for a moment, swimming in the pain and feeling as if he'd go under, but he didn't. Adrenaline flooded his body. He rolled and came up out of it, raising his glove as much to see if he'd caught the ball as to make a play, and there it was, nestled in the brown leather like an egg in its nest.

Reaction took over. Josh didn't even think about the throw he needed to make—he just threw it.

The runner on third was halfway home. He spun to recover his base, but Josh fired the ball to the third baseman, who caught it and fired it in turn to the second baseman before his runner could get back, either.

The crowd went silent as they absorbed what had happened and took the time to process what they'd just seen: a triple play. Game over. Syracuse Titans, 7, Toledo Nighthawks, 6.

The Titan players ran screaming at Josh and picked him up despite his pleas. Once he was up on their shoulders, he forgot about the pain and instead rode his teammates like a genie on some magic carpet, floating across the field and soaking up the joy of victory and the treasure that was waiting for him.

The celebration didn't last.

Josh's mom went wild when she saw him up close, and she insisted they go directly to the hospital, which was only five minutes up the street. Nurses and doctors— not unused to treating knife and gunshot wounds in the city's emergency room—cringed at the sight of Josh. He wanted to look in a mirror, but they stuck an IV into his arm and told him it would be best if he didn't.

"Let me give you something for the pain, honey," a young nurse said, putting her hand on his arm as she injected something into his IV.

Within a few minutes Josh began to float, and it didn't even bother him that they had taken off his clothes and put him into a gown. Before he knew it, they laid him down on a table and rolled him into a plastic capsule that made him think of a space coffin. The machine whirred and banged, but Josh felt no pain with the shot he'd been given. Finally the machine spit him out. They wheeled him down the hall, not back to the emergency room, but into a regular hospital room where his parents stood holding hands beside the bed, talking quietly with a doctor.

"Hi," Josh said, reading the worried expressions on their faces as the doctor slipped out of the room. Two nurses helped him into the bed.

His mom grasped his hand and squeezed tight enough that Josh could feel it.

"Everything's going to be okay," she said.

"Then how come you're crying?" Josh asked.

She nodded and said, "They just want to keep an eye on you overnight, to make sure the bleeding stops, honey."

"What bleeding?" Josh asked cheerfully, his words sounding slurred and the pain a distant memory. "Where's Benji and Jaden?"

"They're outside in the waiting room," his mom said. "They'll be in once we get you settled."

"You fractured your orbital," his dad said. "The part of the skull around the eye socket. You should be fine. They just don't want to take any chances because of the eye."

"It's just an eye," Josh said, giggling. "That's why you got two of them, right?"

The look on his mother's face made him laugh even more. Then something came to him through the fog.

"Hey, I'm gonna be okay to play in the Hall of Fame Tournament, right, Dad?" he said.

His parents looked at each other and his dad said, "The doctor went to look at the MRI, Josh. It'll be a few minutes."

"A few minutes for what?" Josh asked, the hot syrup of panic filling his chest and starting to spread, despite the shot.

"Easy, buddy," his dad said as Josh struggled to sit up.

"Nurse," his mom called at the door. "Can you come here, please? He's a little excited."

"Dad?"

His father took his hand and placed the other on Josh's chest, nearly spanning it and gently laying him back down.

"I can play, right?" Josh asked.

"We don't know, Josh," his father said. "Maybe not."

CHAPTER EIGHT

EVEN THOUGH THE DRUGS kept the pain partially at bay, the dull throb behind Josh's eye didn't go away. His left eye was swollen completely shut. He was getting used to seeing out of just the right eye. He and his mom and dad sat in a doctor's office at the Golisano Children's Hospital in Syracuse. Dr. Cohen was a wiry man with tan skin, dark black hair, and glasses that hung halfway down his nose. He removed the X-rays from a big manila envelope and clipped the first two up on a light box that hung on the wall.

Using a pointer to trace the dark eye socket hole in Josh's skull before detouring along a thin gray line, he said, "So, as you can see, this is the fracture, dangerously close to the optic nerve. One way to heal this is to just let nature run its course. Stay away from any kind of sports or contact for another five or six weeks and this should mend enough to stabilize the area. Or, we can go in and fix it."

"I sure can't wait five more weeks," Josh said. "The Hall of Fame National Championship Tournament is in three weeks. You got to fix it."

Dr. Cohen looked down at him and blinked. "I understand. I used to play third base myself."

"You think you can fix this?" Josh's dad asked.

"And keep him safe," his mother said, folding her arms across her chest. "That is a must. We are *not* going to do something that could jeopardize Josh's eyesight in any way."

Dr. Cohen nodded. "The procedure I'm thinking about won't jeopardize his sight. I would never do that. If anything, this will be safer for him. He could fall down the stairs or slip in the shower, and if he hits that bone again, he'd damage the optic nerve. That we don't want. That could cost him the eye. What I'm talking about would stabilize the area. Basically putting a small metal patch over the crack and screwing it down into the bone on either side. It would be very secure.

"But," Dr. Cohen said, wincing, "there's more to consider."

"I knew it," Josh's mother said, slapping her hand on the arm of her chair.

"Nothing medical," Dr. Cohen said, holding up a hand. "It would be cosmetic."

"Cosmetic?" Josh said. "I don't even know what that means."

"Appearance," Dr. Cohen said. "You'd have a scar on your face. With what I'd have to do, there's no way around it."

"A scar?" his mom said, horrified. "You're kidding."

"It's the only option," the doctor said. "Very safe. Medically sound. I could run the incision along the natural line under the eye so it wouldn't be too bad. Eventually, it will probably fade away so much you'd hardly notice, but there's no way around it."

"I don't care about a scar," Josh said. "I want to play. I *have* to play. Dad, we can win this thing."

Josh wanted to tell his father that he knew about Nike and the contract and that he'd do anything to help, but he knew he shouldn't, so he thought up something else.

"There'll be college scouts there," Josh said. "Mom, you want me to go to college. That's all you talk about. This is my dream."

"No. We can't do this," she said, standing up. "You can't have a scar."

"Mom, who *cares*?" Josh said, clasping his hands together as if in prayer.

"You might not care now," she said, "but that's what God made parents for. Come on, Gary. Dr. Cohen, thank you, but no thank you."

"I can't sit around for five weeks and miss this tournament," Josh said.

"Him sitting around is going to drive us all crazy," Josh's dad said.

"This is a once-in-a-lifetime chance," Josh said. "It's a national championship. It's in Cooperstown! Dad? Tell her!"

Josh's father didn't get up. He sat with his legs splayed out to the sides, staring at the X-ray. Finally he cleared his throat, looked up at Josh's mom, and said, "You heard him, Laura. This is the safest thing we could do."

"The safest thing is to have him sit out for five weeks and let this thing heal without a scar," his mom said, raising her voice loud enough that Josh could feel it in his eye.

Dr. Cohen looked back and forth between Josh's parents. "This is something you should all discuss by yourselves."

"There's no discussion," Josh's dad said. "We're doing it. It's the safest thing."

"And he can play *base*ball," his mom said, spitting it out like some four-letter word.

"It's his dream," Josh's father said.

"His dream?" his mom said. "Or *yours*?"

His mom turned and stormed out of the doctor's office.

"You sure you want this, Son?" Josh's dad asked.

"Please, Dad," Josh said. "Please let me play."

His father looked deep into Josh's eyes, and Josh

thought for an instant that his dad might spill a tear. Then his dad nodded. "Okay, we'll do it."

"Thank you, Dad," Josh said, grabbing his father's thick arm. "Thank you so much."

Dr. Cohen cleared his throat and said, "I can do the surgery this week, but I'd really like you to get your wife on board with this."

"She gets excited," his dad said in a low rumble. "Don't worry, Doc. I'll handle Laura. Let's get it done."

CHAPTER NINE

WITH SCHOOL IN ITS final few days, the noise in the Grant Middle School cafeteria rivaled that of any place on Earth. Chatter sprinkled with hoots, catcalls, shrieks, and howls of laughter always left Josh's ears buzzing when he finished eating his lunch and headed for his next class.

"Man, you're like Ronnie Lott!" Benji said above the noise, tearing his ham sandwich free from the cellophane and stuffing half of it into his mouth.

"Who's Ronnie Lott?" Jaden asked, cracking open her carton of milk and taking a sip before she opened her notebook to a page packed with columns and tiny symbols.

"Oh man," Benji said, speaking around the huge wad of bread and ham filling his mouth, "just when I think you're not such a girl. Ronnie Lott's a famous football player from the eighties."

"I *am* a girl, Lido," Jaden said, slapping her notebook and straightening her back. "I like being a girl. Girls rule, right, Josh?"

Josh felt the pulse in the dull pain behind his eye quicken. He looked down at his meat loaf sandwich and mumbled, "Jeez, I can't win this one. You two fight it out."

"Anyway," Jaden said, nibbling on an apple, "who is he, and why is Josh like some old football player?"

"Well, you know, with my dad being a pro ballplayer himself," Benji said through his food, "I get all the good stories. So, Ronnie Lott played for the Forty-niners back when they were a dynasty. They were on their way to the Super Bowl, but Lott crushed his finger, and they said there was no way he could play with it the way it was. Too risky for infection or something like that."

Even though Benji didn't live with his dad, he never missed an opportunity to talk about him, a big, burly plastics factory worker who played offensive lineman for the semipro Syracuse Express on autumn afternoons.

"So?" Jaden said. "So, he crushed his finger?"

Benji swallowed his wad of food and leaned forward. "So? So, he cut it off!"

"What?" Jaden said in disgust.

"Whop!" Benji said with a chopping motion. "Cut the

finger right off, just so he could play in the playoffs and help his team win. Same thing with Josh. Whop!"

Benji made a dramatic slicing motion under his eye.

"Did he really?" Josh asked, his chest flooding with pride at the comparison. "I think I've heard of Ronnie Lott."

"Josh Lott, that's what I'll start calling you," Benji said, jamming the other half of the sandwich into his mouth and nodding furiously.

Josh gently patted the swollen skin beneath his eye, which had surprised him that morning by allowing in a slit of light. "I guess."

"Wow," Jaden said, obviously impressed. "I hate to say it, but you're right, Lido. Maybe I could do a story on this for the *Post-Standard*. Get some pictures of that eye or the scar right after they cut you. People love to read that kind of stuff."

"Gosh," Josh said.

"I was going to put something together about this," Jaden said, patting her notebook.

"What's that?" Benji asked through his food.

"Basically, it shows why out of the teams that have qualified so far, the Syracuse Titans have a great chance to win that Hall of Fame Tournament," Jaden said, obviously proud. "See? It's all the statistics of all the different teams. I rate the pitchers, the defense, batting, everything every team that qualified has done over the past six months. Then, look, I add a value to all these things and calculate it out. The Titans are definitely the team to beat. That's what I was thinking the headline of my story could be: 'The Team to Beat.' It's a good follow-up to 'The Triple Play,' don't you think?"

"Where did you get all that stuff?" Josh asked, leaning over as he finished off his sandwich.

"I'm a reporter, Josh," she said. "I've got my sources. Well, mostly just the internet. But do you realize, with you guys being the team to beat and you having this surgery just so you can play, the Titans could make some national news?"

Josh raised his eyebrows.

"I mean it," Jaden said.

Benji almost choked on his food and took a big swig of milk to wash it down before he gasped and said, "Man, Josh, I can see it, you and me on the front page of *SI for Kids*. Maybe even a piece on *SportsCenter*. I mean, we win the national championship and that, like, makes us famous, right?"

"You and Josh?" Jaden said, squinting at Benji.

"Me being the other heavy hitter on the team," Benji said. "The Dynamic Duo, something like that."

"But Lido," Jaden said with wonder, "you haven't hit a single home run this season."

"Well," Benji said, wrinkling his brow before snapping his finger. "Batman and Robin, then. He's the bat man knocking it out of the park, and I'm robbin' bases all over the place. Get it?"

"You have, like, two steals in the past two months," Jaden said.

"Yeah, see? I'm Robin, out there stealin' bases," Benji said with a deadly serious look. "Why do you have to get all caught up in numbers all the time, anyway? I thought you wanted to win a Pulitzer one day. Don't you have to be, like, creative to do that? Use your creativity here, will you?"

The bell rang. They picked up their garbage and headed for the hall.

"I think I'll stick with the Ronnie Lott angle," Jaden said. "Josh taking a scar for the team. Besides, there's still one more team to qualify for the tournament from out on the West Coast, so I have to wait for them to be completely accurate with my numbers. I've got a study hall eighth period. I think I'll text my editor at the *Post-Standard*. I'll let you guys know what he says in history."

With English, math, and Spanish between lunch and history—as well as the constant worry about having his face cut open in two days' time—Josh forgot all about Jaden's newspaper story until he saw her and Benji huddled up outside their last class of the day, having a serious discussion.

"Hey," he said, noticing the expression on Jaden's face, "what's up? Editor didn't like the idea?"

"Well, he liked it," Jaden said. "I mean, he gets it, you being the big star of the team and doing what you're doing, but . . ."

"Yeah?" Josh said, nearly laughing at her look of distress.

"Well," Jaden said, looking down and shaking her head, "I don't think you're exactly going to be the big story I thought you were, Josh. I know you don't care too much about that stuff anyway, so that's good."

"What are you talking about?" Josh asked as the bell to class rang. "Why wouldn't I?"

"There's a bigger story happening in the Hall of Fame Tournament," Jaden said. "It's a *huge* story. You'll hear about it. It'll be on the news. I mean, *I* can't believe it myself."

"I'll *hear* it? What are you talking about?" Josh asked. "Come on, you guys, just tell me!"

CHAPTER TEN

"I WAS WRONG," JADEN said with a worried look. "You're not the favorite team to win anymore."

"What," Josh said, chuckling, "your numbers weren't right? That's no big deal."

"*We're* no big deal," Benji said, sulking.

"What do you mean, 'We're no big deal'?" Josh asked.

"*SportsCenter*? Batman and Robin? Poof," Benji said. "Up in smoke."

"Enough with the riddles," Josh said, "and tell me what you're talking about."

"Mickey Mullen Junior," Jaden said.

"Mickey Mullen? Who, the baseball player?" Josh asked.

"No. The former Boston Red Sox Hall of Famer, three-time Cy Young Award winner, star of *Baseball*

Nights, *Crossfire*, and *Bloody Monday* Mickey Mullen," Benji said. "*That* Mickey Mullen."

"But who's Mickey Mullen Junior?" Josh asked.

"He's not so junior," Benji said. "He's as big as you."

"That's the story," Jaden said. "It's Mickey's son. I never even knew Mickey Mullen had a son who played. The team's from LA."

"And they're the last team from the West Coast you were talking about?" Josh said.

"Right," Jaden said.

"Yeah, they won some tournament championship game in Newport last night," Benji said. "And now this guy's stealing our thunder."

"Still," Jaden said, "you have to admit, it's pretty exciting. I mean, you get to go up against a guy whose dad is a legend. They say Mickey Junior is following right in his footsteps, too."

The bell rang for class. Josh felt his mouth drop open as that sinking feeling returned.

When Josh got home, he found his father under the kitchen sink, banging on the disposal with a wrench.

"I swear," his father said, wriggling out of the cabinet and struggling to sit up. "I can't wait. Hey, killer. How's the face?"

"Hurts," Josh said, setting his backpack down on the kitchen table and puffing up with pride. His dad had never called him "killer" before, and Josh suspected it was because of how he was handling his injury. "Can't wait for what?"

His dad raised an eyebrow. "Oh, nothing. Hire a plumber, I guess."

"Why don't you?" Josh asked.

His dad shrugged. "Oh, you know. Being careful is all. Don't worry, we're fine. It's just that you don't get to save up too much money playing in the minors. That's why—even though she *is* overreacting about this surgery thing—your mom's right about college."

Josh nodded and took the milk out of the fridge to pour himself a glass. A plate of his mom's oatmeal cookies was sitting on the table.

"Hey," Josh said, "did you hear about Mickey Mullen?"

Josh's dad scooped up his tools and dropped them noisily into his metal toolbox.

"Oh, that," he said. "It might make the tournament like this grease on my hands—messy, but we'll get the job done. You gotta be confident. Besides, it's a good thing for the tournament."

"Why?" Josh asked, taking a cookie.

"Money makes the world go round," his father said, drying his hands. "That's why."

Josh set the cookie back down on the plate and said, "Money?"

"A tournament needs sponsors, like Nike and Pepsi, and a TV contract with ESPN," his dad said. "That's the real world."

His father stared at him for a moment, seeing if he got it before he said, "The organizers are trying to make this the biggest thing in Little League Baseball—bigger than the Little League World Series, bigger than the Junior Olympics—and they're on their way, so a guy like Mickey Mullen shows up with his son? Please. That's a no-brainer."

"I don't know why you're so casual about it," Josh said. "I thought we really want to win this thing."

"Of course I want to win."

"And his son's supposed to be good," Josh said. "Benji said he's as big as I am."

At nearly six feet tall, Josh had only heard of one other twelve-year-old bigger than he was, and that kid played basketball for Bishop Ludden, the Catholic school on the west side.

"He is," his dad said, turning his back to Josh so he could wash his hands in the sink. "Supposed to be a heck of a player, too. Pitcher, like his old man."

"You think they could beat us?"

"Anyone could beat us," his dad said, "but if we're the best, we'll win. I told you before, you can't be afraid of a good rival, and this Mickey Junior may be the best rival you've ever seen. You should be chomping at the bit to step up to the plate against this guy. You'll have to be at your best."

"I am chomping at the bit," Josh said. "I'm having the operation, aren't I? I have to do this."

His father studied him for a minute before he said, "You don't *have* to, Josh. Don't think that. You never *have* to play. That's the beauty of sports. You play because you *want* to. You love to."

"I do," Josh said.

"Good," his father said with a nod, picking his tools back up.

"Where you going?" Josh asked.

"The roof," his dad said, "to start getting some new shingles put on before dinner so we can lose that blue tarp. I've got practice right after we eat."

"You mean *we've* got practice," Josh said.

"No, not we, I," his dad said. "You're not going."

Josh felt his heart skip a beat. "Why?"

"Your face," his dad said. "It looks so bad it's hurting me."

"Gee, thanks."

His father grinned. "I'm kidding. I don't want you even around a baseball until it's totally safe. You just take it easy, we'll get this operation behind us, you'll heal up, and we'll go win that thing."

"You really think we can win it?" Josh asked. "Even against the LA Comets with Mickey Mullen's son pitching?"

A worried look passed across his father's face like the shadow of an airplane before he said, "I told you. You gotta be confident to win."

CHAPTER ELEVEN

JOSH HAD HIS OPERATION. The healing process seemed to take forever, especially with him having to watch practices from behind the backstop until the stitches could come out. On the Saturday morning the week before the tournament, he finally had the stitches removed. His dad took him out to their practice field, only not with the rest of the team. It was just the two of them. From his duffel bag, Josh's dad removed a dark blue foam mask that looked like something a hockey goalie might wear.

"Here," his dad said, "try it on."

Josh gave him a quizzical look.

"It was part of the deal I cut with your mom," his dad said. "You get to play, but only if you wear the mask. Don't even start with me. She's worried about you. That's why we love her."

Josh put on the mask and tugged his cap down, then

stepped up to the plate. His father carried a basket of balls to the mound.

"Okay," his dad said. "Let's make sure you're over it."

"I am, Dad," Josh said, huffing. "I told you a hundred times."

"I know what you said," his father said, "but you took a heck of a shot. I want to make sure you can stand there and read a pitch. Your vision is your gift. There aren't many players who can see the ball the way you can, but getting hit like that can be a distraction, even to a major-league player."

Josh nodded and readied his bat. His father—who had pitched for thirteen years in the minor leagues—wound up and let one fly. Josh blinked and lost it. He swung and missed. The ball clanged into the metal backstop.

"You okay?" his dad asked.

"Fine," Josh said. "Just pitch it."

His father threw three more pitches, and Josh missed them all. His eyes began to fill with tears. He brushed one back and ground his teeth. His father left the mound and put an arm around his shoulder.

"Relax," he said. "You're trying too hard. It might take some time."

"No," Josh said, wagging his head angrily. "It can't. I'm ready. Give me another, Dad. Please."

His father sighed, but returned to the mound. When Josh stepped into the batter's box, his dad wound up again.

CHAPTER TWELVE

JOSH WIDENED HIS EYES, forcing them to stay open. He concentrated so hard that the pitch passed him by without him even swinging.

"What happened?" his father asked.

"I'm okay!" Josh shouted. "I saw it! I didn't swing, but I didn't blink, either."

"Good," his father said, grinning wide.

Josh nicked the next pitch, dribbling it to the mound, then lit into the one after that, driving it into the hole between first and second. The next one he hammered, sending it over the fence. His father grinned and kept them coming. Pitch after pitch, he threw and Josh hammered them all. When the basket of balls was empty, his father jogged to home plate, hugged him, and swung him in the air.

"You did it, Josh!" his father said. "You're ready."

When they got back home, Josh's parents took his little sister, him, and his friends to Green Lakes State Park for the afternoon. They took over a picnic table and spread a big blanket out on the grass overlooking the aqua green water that sparkled like a gem under the hot sun. Josh's dad played *The Eagles' Greatest Hits* on their boom box while he drank a soda and flipped sizzling burgers on the iron grill.

Josh's mom took his sister down to the water while Josh lay between his two friends, looking up through the orange glow of his eyelids at the sunspots drifting across his vision. His skin baked comfortably, cooled from time to time by a fretful breeze. Jaden started chattering about Mickey Mullen Jr., a topic she'd been on all week, and one he didn't relish hearing about.

"How do you know he's so good?" Josh said. "You keep talking about his statistics, but you haven't actually *seen* him play. He might not be so great. He might just be playing against easy teams."

That seemed to quiet her down. Josh gently dabbed at the gauze his mom had insisted on taping to his face to protect the healing wound from the sun, even though it was pretty well healed. Jaden's silence on the subject of Mickey Mullen Jr. and the comfort of lying in the heat made Josh sigh. Laughter and music from the crowded park around them blended into a lulling symphony; Josh thought he might even fall asleep.

That's when Benji's stomach gurgled.

"Can't wait to tear into those burgers," Benji said dreamily.

"Hey Jaden," Josh said, his own eyes still closed. "You think I can keep my batting average up over five hundred in this tournament?"

"Maybe. Who knows?" Jaden said, yawning and nudging him with an elbow hard enough to make him sit up. "Hey, put some on my back, will you? I'm turning over. Time to get some work done."

Jaden handed him a bottle of lotion and scooted her butt around on the towel, holding the wild shock of hair up off her back so he could spread the creamy lotion on her bronze shoulders. Josh stole a look at Benji, who was grinning up at him, puckering his lips, and winking. Josh shook his head and lathered her back up anyway.

"What work?" Josh asked as Jaden opened the school backpack she'd brought along with her.

"This," she said, removing several books that he recognized as biographies on Mickey Mullen, "and this and this."

She added several magazines to the pile before taking out her notebook and pen, adjusting her white plastic sunglasses, and then settling onto her stomach.

"I get *SI for Kids*," Josh said, sitting up and shading his eyes from the sun. "But *Teen Beat*? What's that got to do with baseball?"

"Background for Mickey Junior," Jaden said somberly. "There's articles on him in both of them."

"What, like dating Taylor Swift?" Benji said, grinning and slapping his round belly.

"No, they're just friends," Jaden said, opening one of the magazines.

"Wait," Benji said, sitting straight, "you've got to be kidding. You're not serious."

"That's the headline. 'Mickey Jr. and Taylor, Just Friends.'"

"I'm barfing," Benji said. "Better slow down on those burgers, Mr. LeBlanc. I am so sick of hearing you talk about Mickey Mullen and his mullet-head son."

"Mullet head," Josh said, laughing. "That's a good one, Benji."

"Why's he a mullet head?" Jaden asked, casting a fiery look at Benji and then Josh.

"Because he is," Benji said, lying back and stuffing a pair of mirrored sunglasses on his face.

"Maybe he wouldn't be such a mullet head if we didn't have to hear about him twenty-four seven," Josh said.

"Hopefully I'll get to ask him about Taylor Swift myself," Jaden said, biting down on her pen and nodding, obviously choosing to ignore Benji and him. "I put a request in through the newspaper to their PR person to sit down with him. I should be hearing back anytime. Think how big that would be!"

"Oh, right," Benji said, staring up at the sun and speaking in a tone of complete boredom. "Like they'll talk to you."

"They might," Jaden said without looking up at Benji. "I already heard back from the tournament's PR person, and she said the Mullens are going to be giving the media all kinds of access during this thing, even the local media. That's me, right? So . . . "

Benji whipped off his glasses and fired an annoyed look at Josh.

Josh shrugged, screwed on the cap to the suntan lotion, and lay back down. He listened to Jaden snapping through her pages and to Benji's increasingly hostile stomach until his dad said the burgers were ready. His dad put the burgers out in the middle of the table with everything else before he went off to retrieve Josh's mom and sister.

Jaden jumped up and slipped on her sandals before putting on a big T-shirt to cover her pink bathing suit.

"Where you going?" Benji said.

"You ever hear of washing your hands, Lido?" she said before marching off toward the bathrooms.

"Your hands don't get dirty if you don't read those trashy magazines," Benji called after her.

"Forget it, Benji," Josh said. "Let's eat."

"She gets me so crazy with all that Mickey Mullen *junk*," Benji said, picking two burgers off the plate with his bare fingers and slapping them down on a bun. "Aren't you sick of it?"

"Kind of," Josh said, watching Jaden disappear among the crowd. "Actually, yes. A lot, but I guess she's just excited about writing the story."

"You notice how all of a sudden she's not so interested in your game?" Benji said, slathering ketchup on his burgers, capping them off with the top bun, and raising an eyebrow at him before taking a huge bite. "I mean, you ask her about your batting average and all she can do is have you rub suntan oil on her back."

"Kind of."

"Yeah, why?" Benji said through his food. "I'll tell you, because she's in love with this Mickey Junior. It's not the *story* and her Pulitzer Prize. She thinks she's Taylor Swift."

Anger and resentment swirled in Josh's stomach, but he said nothing.

"Hey," Benji said, letting go of his burgers and fishing his cell phone out of his bathing suit pocket. "Didn't Jaden say her dad had to work, like, some twelve-hour shift? I got an idea. How do you block the number you're calling from?"

"Dial star sixty-seven, then the number," Josh said, watching Benji dial.

"Remember that voice you'd make when we made fun of that mean bus driver we used to have?" Benji asked.

"Sure," Josh said. "Remember we fooled her own husband with it?"

The muted ring from Jaden's phone sounded off from inside her backpack beside the picnic table's leg.

"Okay," Benji said, handing Josh his phone, "use that voice. I'll tell you exactly what to say."

CHAPTER THIRTEEN

JOSH'S PARENTS RETURNED WITH his little sister. His dad put Laurel into a high chair that clipped onto the side of the picnic table and his mom began to feed her chunks of hamburger, half of which she tossed about the table and grass.

"Now, that's what I call quality grub," Benji said, slapping his naked gut and burping loudly. "Excuse me."

"Thank you for the burgers, Mr. LeBlanc," Jaden said, wiping her mouth on a napkin, "and the potato salad was delicious, Mrs. LeBlanc. Thank you for lunch."

"You have very nice manners," Josh's mom said to Jaden, patting her arm.

Benji rolled his eyes at Josh and pretended to stick a finger down his throat. It wasn't often that someone beat him to the punch on manners. Then Benji pointed, silently clapping with delight as Jaden returned to the blanket and took the cell phone out of her pack.

Josh turned his attention to Jaden too, and a feeling of dread crept into his bones as he realized they'd probably taken things too far. She stood listening to the message on her phone, the excitement building on her face until she bounced up and down and squealed.

"Oh my gosh," she said, holding the phone out and looking at it like it was a friend. "Oh my gosh! I've got to get to New York City! Mr. LeBlanc, I hate to ask you, but my dad has rounds until midnight, and I have to get there."

"Why do you have to get to New York, dear?" Josh's mom asked.

"Oh my gosh," Jaden said, jumping up and down, "I just got a call from Mickey Mullen's publicist. They're in New York and he agreed to give me an interview. They saw my request and were so impressed with a twelve-year-old girl writing for a newspaper—that's what they said—and he's in New York for some movie thing and some time freed up on his schedule and they said all I have to do is *get* there."

"We've got a dinner with my assistant coaches and their wives tonight, Jaden," Josh's dad said, "so I can't take you, even if your dad would let you go."

"Hey," Benji said, pointing to the family at the next picnic table over from them, "I heard those people talking. They're *from* New York. I heard them talking about how they were leaving early to beat the traffic back into the city. You should just ask them."

Jaden didn't even hesitate. She marched right over to them.

"Jaden?" Josh's mom said. "You can't just—"

But Jaden didn't hear. She was on a mission. The father of the small family was tall and skinny with pale skin gone beet red from the sun. He stood chewing on a cucumber as he flipped a rack of vegetables on his grill. His wife, a heavy woman wearing a white one-piece bathing suit with the face of a duck on her big tummy, guzzled down a Dr Pepper as she fed Twinkies to her screaming twin boys.

"Hi, folks," Jaden said, her Texas drawl coming out the way it did when she got nervous or excited, talking fast, without even thinking, "I hate to interrupt, but my friend happened to overhear that you all are from New York City and heading back today and I really would like to just catch a ride down there with you all if you don't mind. I know it's a strange thing to ask someone you don't even know, but I have an interview with Mickey Mullen—you know, the baseball player and movie star—that I have to get there for. I mean, I'd have to get permission from my dad and all, but you've got kids of your own so maybe he'd say yes, you never know. I mean, this is like a once-in-a-lifetime deal. So, do you think you could help me?"

The big woman blinked at Jaden while one of the little boys pawed at her leg, mewling for another Twinkie.

"Eddy?" she said accusingly to her husband. "Do you know this girl?"

The husband let the hand with the cucumber fall to his side as he shook his head.

"Are you on drugs?" the big woman asked.

"No," Jaden said, stammering. "I just . . . It's just that—"

"We're from Schenectady," the lady said.

"I . . ." Jaden said, pointing back toward Benji, "are you sure?"

"Are we sure, Eddy?" the wife asked.

"I am," Eddy, the husband, said, his Adam's apple bobbing.

"Oh," Jaden said, her shoulders falling. "I'm awfully sorry."

Jaden marched back toward their picnic table, her face red and tears brimming in her eyes. Benji howled and pointed.

"Did you see that guy's face?" Benji said, laughing. "She's so hot for her Mickey Mullen exclusive that she just asked two complete strangers for a ride."

"What are you two up to?" Josh's mom asked.

Josh shrugged.

Benji grinned and said, "Just kidding around a little."

Jaden stopped in front of Josh. "That was you on my voice mail, wasn't it? There is no Mickey Mullen interview. Yeah, that's how bad I wanted it. You got me to make a complete fool out of myself. Are you proud?"

Josh shrugged and forced a weak laugh. "We were just kidding around."

"From this goofball, I expect it," Jaden said, pointing at Benji, who didn't seem to mind the insult. "But you?"

"It was a joke," Josh said with a weak smile.

Jaden looked at him for a moment, then said, "That stinks."

She turned and just walked away, heading straight for the water, where she waded out to her knees before diving in and disappearing beneath the sparkling surface.

Benji flopped back down on the blanket, still chortling to himself as he plastered the sunglasses onto his face. Josh's dad scooped up a pile of paper plates, cups, and empty cans and headed for a nearby trash can, shaking his head.

Josh turned to his mom and asked, "What should I do?"

She looked up from cleaning his little sister's face and said, "Go tell her you're sorry, Josh."

"We didn't mean anything bad," he said.

His mom gave him a hard look and said, "I saw the way you and Benji acted when she talked about Mickey Mullen and his son, so I don't think you should try to tell me that you didn't mean anything bad. I don't think that's quite truthful."

"Well," Josh said, looking down at the grass and picking a few thin blades with his bare toes before he looked back up. "Do you think she'll forgive me?"

His mom's eyes drifted to the spot where Jaden had disappeared beneath the water's green surface. "I don't know, but she's your good friend, so you better go try."

CHAPTER FOURTEEN

THE VERY NEXT WEEK, their bus pulled into the Beaver Valley Campsite in the pouring rain. The cabins looked dreary on the hillside under the eaves of a dark green woods that carpeted the mountains as far as the eye could see. The bus stopped in a gravel lot next to the main lodge and everyone piled out into the storm, grabbing their duffel bags from under the bus and trudging to their cabins through the puddles.

Jaden and her doctor dad—who had decided to make a vacation out of her writing assignment—headed toward one of the smaller cabins at the far end of the line.

"Can I help you?" Josh asked Jaden, reaching for one of her two big suitcases.

"I got it," she said, snatching it away from him.

Josh stood and watched her go, crestfallen, until she twisted her head around and said, "Thanks anyway, though."

It wasn't much, but Josh was grateful for even a small sign that she had forgiven him for the prank he and Benji had pulled on her at Green Lakes. Since then, things hadn't been the same between them. He was hoping that the time they'd get to spend together during the coming week might change that and get things back to normal. Josh carried his mom's and sister's bags along with his own while his dad held an umbrella to protect his mom and sleeping sister as they walked.

"Use that for Josh," his mom said.

"No, Mom," Josh said. "Why?"

"You've got to keep that incision dry," she said.

"Mom, cut it out. That was until I got the stitches out," he said, tracing a fingertip along the ridge of scar tissue running across his cheekbone. He remembered the color of his face in the mirror that very morning. The bruising had faded over the weeks from a deep purple to a sickly yellow, and the scarlet gash had begun to grow pink. At least his eye worked, and he could play.

His mom gave him a worried look, patting Laurel's head, which was slumped on her shoulder, as she said, "I just don't like it. It looks . . . well, I don't know, very sore. I'm sorry."

"I'm fine, Mom," Josh said. "Really. I haven't even

taken an Advil in over a week. It's all good and I'm ready to go."

"Laura," his father said, taking her by the arm. "Come on. Josh won't melt."

Josh followed, and Benji slogged along beside him without looking up.

Halfway to the cabin, Benji said, "I can't believe you won't give me the top bunk."

"Lido," Josh said, dropping his hand from his face, "you bounced around up there like a monkey the last time we shared a bunk. The springs squeaked in my face all night, and I kept thinking you'd be busting through."

"You can't be a heavy hitter if you're a lightweight," Benji said, stamping in a puddle. "Look at Manny Ramirez. Look at the Babe."

"The Babe? That was back in the thirties," Josh said. "Nutrition was, like, a bacon sandwich."

"Animal protein," Benji said, nodding. "Nothing wrong with that."

"I'm taking top," Josh said.

"All this freaking mud," Benji said, stamping. "I'm gonna have your footprints all over my sleeping bag."

"Just 'cause you stepped on my bed to get to the top doesn't mean I'll do it to you," Josh said. "That's what the ladder is for. I kept telling you that."

"I'd appreciate that courtesy," Benji said in earnest, hurrying now to hold the door open for Josh's family as they wiped their feet on the rope mat of the cabin's front porch.

"Benji, you are such a gentleman," Josh's mom said, holding Laurel tight as she slipped quietly into the cabin to lay her down on the bed.

Josh rolled his eyes.

"See?" Benji said as they shed their wet coats and dumped their bags down inside the tiny back bedroom. "I'm like a magnet for women."

"That's my mom, Lido."

Benji shrugged. "I'm just saying. You can't turn it on and off—you're either suave or you're not."

"Suave?" Josh said, unrolling his sleeping bag on the striped mattress of the top bunk. "That's like a shampoo."

"Suave means smooth," Benji said. "Sophisticated. Stylish. Hip. A chick magnet."

"Lido," Josh said, "sometimes I think it was you who got hit by a beanball."

In the front room, Josh's mom worked in the tiny kitchenette while his dad stood holding back the curtain and looking out over the baseball field and a murky pond.

"Hope it stops soon so we can get in a little practice after dinner," he said. "Get tuned up for tomorrow."

"You think we'll even play tomorrow?" Josh asked, eyeing the thick gray sky.

"Forecast is sunshine," his dad said. "Depends on if it dries out. This field is a mud hole, but the Dream Park fields are supposed to be the latest and greatest, all sixteen of them. I'm sure they've got good drainage."

"Can we go into town with the guys?" Josh asked. "Someone said the camp has a shuttle bus that goes every hour, and we want to see the Hall of Fame."

"Sure," his dad said. "I'd go with you, but I promised your mom I'd help get unpacked. You guys just be back by dinner."

"I don't know," Josh's mom said, turning from the refrigerator and wringing her hands. "Maybe you should rest."

"Mom, seriously. Cut it out," Josh said. "I'm going to look like a freak out there as it is; you don't have to treat me like one."

"You're not going to look like a freak," his mom said, referring to the dark blue padded mask that would protect his face. "You'll look like a child with parents who care about his health and well-being."

"Actually," Benji said, "you kinda look like Jason from *Texas Chainsaw Massacre*."

Everyone turned to stare at Benji.

"No, but I mean in a good way," Benji said, blushing and holding up his hands. "Like you'll scare the other team. I mean, in a good way. Scare, like, intimidate them. Give us that winning edge. You need an edge, right, Coach LeBlanc? You say that, right?"

Josh's dad sighed heavily. "That's right, Benji."

Benji nodded proudly.

"Come on," Josh said.

"Take the umbrella," Josh's mom said. "And you two

make sure you ask Jaden. She's your friend, and you don't want her feeling uncomfortable with all these boys."

"Of course," Josh said, leading Benji by the arm. "Not that you have to worry about Jaden."

"She's very shy," his mom said.

"Yeah, but she's never uncomfortable," Josh said, creaking open the cabin door and stepping out onto the porch before snapping open the umbrella. "She doesn't care what anyone thinks."

"You better believe that," Benji said, scooping up his Red Sox hat and following Josh out the door. "I told her she shouldn't pull her hair back like that and she told me if she wanted my opinion, she'd submit a request in writing. So far, nothing."

"Nothing what?" Josh asked.

"In writing."

Josh studied his friend's face for a moment before Benji pointed over his shoulder and said, "Hey, look. Jaden."

They slogged through puddles along the gravel path following Jaden toward the main lodge, shouting her name over the steady hiss of rain until she pulled up short in a shiny red raincoat with a hood.

"Hey, guys," she said, looking slightly nervous. "What's up?"

"We were gonna come get you," Josh said. "Baseball Hall of Fame is what's up."

"Picture with me next to the Babe's statue," Benji said. "Kind of a next-generation thing. You know, heavy hitter from the past and the future. Figure I can market signed copies on eBay."

"Oh," Jaden said.

"It was a joke, really," Benji said, obviously disappointed not to get a rise out of Jaden.

"I'm gonna get mine with Hank Aaron. Hammering Hank," Josh said. "That's my man."

"Nice," Jaden said stiffly.

"Hey," Josh said, pointing toward the driveway of the main lodge.

In front of the shabby-looking, powder blue shuttle bus—with "Beaver Valley Campsite" painted in chipped letters on the side—rested a long, sleek limousine. The car glowed white like a spaceship with smoky windows trimmed in little blue lights and the rain spattering uselessly off it.

"I wonder who that's for," Benji said.

Jaden glanced over and bit her lower lip. "Umm, I think it's for me."

"You?" Benji said.

"You're kidding," Josh said. "What for?"

CHAPTER FIFTEEN

BEFORE JADEN COULD ANSWER, a man in black livery wearing a driver's cap and tie slipped out of the limousine and strode their way with an umbrella.

"Would you happen to be Miss Neidermeyer?" the man asked with a British accent, his mouth showing off strong white teeth beneath a silver mustache.

"Yes," Jaden said.

"Quite right," the man said, moving the umbrella to shield her from the rain. "This way please, Miss."

Benji laughed and stared in disbelief. "You gotta be kidding me."

"There's a press conference," Jaden said, a spark in her eye. "So, despite your bad joke, I am going to get to interview Mickey Mullen after all."

"You're taking a limo?" Josh said.

"They sent it," Jaden said.

"Who?" Josh asked.

Jaden's honey-colored face flushed. "Well, I think it's the tournament, but it might be the Comets."

"Yes, Miss," the chauffeur said, "the Comets, and we do need to get going. We're picking up several newspaper reporters who'll be flying in from Los Angeles with the Mullens."

"There's no airport," Josh said, wrinkling his eyes at the driver.

The driver cleared his throat and said, "There's a *private* airfield. Miss?"

"I thought you're supposed to be covering *our* team?" Benji said, casting an angry look at Jaden, then the driver. "These guys are from halfway across the globe."

"Bud Poliquin, my editor at the *Post-Standard*, said that he'd love to have me do a story on the Comets if I got the chance," Jaden said. "Come on, Benji, be serious, it's *Mickey Mullen*."

"Mullen, shmullen," Benji said, turning to walk away. "Come on, Josh. Let's go see the Babe's statue."

Josh followed Benji toward the shuttle bus, watching Jaden as the driver held the door for her so she could slip inside the limo. He and Benji climbed the stairs and found a husky lady with glasses and a Red Sox cap chomping gum behind the wheel of the shuttle bus.

"Hey," Benji said brightly, touching his cap. "Go, Red Sox, right?"

"Welcome aboard the Beaver Valley Campsite shuttle," she said without expression, banging the doors shut with a hand lever. "Bus picks up in town every hour. No gum, candy, food, or drinks allowed on the bus. No standing up. No pictures inside the bus 'cause those flashes drive me nuts."

"We're going to the Baseball Hall of Fame, please," Josh said as they sat down in a torn seat.

"Just one stop," the grumpy lady said, blowing a bubble and firing up the engine. "In the center of town. It's not too far, though."

"Couldn't you just swing by there?" Benji said with his most winning grin. "That rain's coming down in buckets. For a fellow Sox fan and all."

The driver swung around and glared at him. "This look like a taxicab to you? It's a shuttle bus. Yeah, I love the Sox. A lot of people do. I got two eyes and two ears like you, too. That doesn't mean I'm taking you home for dinner."

The smile on Benji's face melted.

"You believe that?" Benji said, thumping his head against the glass as the limo pulled away. "Jaden's doing *Lifestyles of the Rich and Famous* while we're stuck with this crazy old bat. Some friend."

"Come on, Lido," Josh said. "What do you want her to do? You'd take a ride in that thing if they asked you."

"I'll have my own limo before you know it," Benji

said, grumbling and pulling his cap down low. "I don't need a ride in anyone else's."

The bus pulled out after the long white limo, but they quickly lost sight of it as the bus rattled slowly along. When they pulled into a grocery store, Benji sat up straight and gripped the seat back in front of them.

"Hey, what's up, lady?" he asked.

The driver adjusted her cap and stepped down off the bus. "Gotta pick up a few things. You two just sit tight."

"Jeez," Benji said, watching her. "You get that? She can't drop us at the Hall of Fame, but she can stop for groceries. You gotta be kidding me."

"We'll get there," Josh said, resting his chin on the seat back.

When the driver finally emerged carrying two cartons of milk in a plastic bag, Benji slapped his hand on the seat. As they drove into town, Benji pointed at an old brick building. "There it is! Hey, lady, just let us out."

"No unauthorized stops," she said without looking back.

The bus continued on for two more blocks and pulled to a stop at the curb where several rain-drenched visitors stood waiting under an awning. Josh followed Benji down the aisle to get off the bus. At the bottom step, Benji turned around.

"Lady," Benji said, "honestly? It's people like you who give Red Sox fans a bad name."

"And you two brats can find your own way back," the driver said. "I don't have to take your abuse."

"Whatever," Benji said, stepping down and flicking his hand in the air.

"Lido," Josh said, hustling to catch up. "You screwball. Now how are we going to get back?"

"Stop worrying," Benji said, flipping his hood up over his hat. "Let's just get there."

They trudged silently through the rain, back up the street leading to the Hall of Fame. When they arrived, they saw that not one but seven stretch limousines had arrived. A small crowd of people was moving through the courtyard and in through the center of three arched entryways.

"There she is," Benji said, "at the front of the line, Miss Fancy Pants, all snug and dry."

To change the subject, as they got into line Josh pointed up at the faded brick building and said, "Just look at it, Lido. The Hall of Fame. Everyone who loves baseball comes to this place. Everyone in the world."

"Yeah," Benji said, looking around. "I could use a hot dog or something."

When they got to the ticket booth, the man pushed his glasses up higher on his nose and studied them for a moment before he said, "Sorry, part of the museum's west wing is temporarily closed due to the press conference. You're welcome to come in and see the exhibits that aren't blocked off, but access to the entire museum won't resume until five-thirty."

"Five-thirty?" Josh said, turning to Benji. "That's too late. We've got to be back by dinner, and we don't even know how we're getting back."

"Can we see the Babe's statue?" Benji asked, his hands plastered against the window of the ticket booth.

"And Hammering Hank's," Josh said.

"Uhh," the man said, running his finger over a map he had in front of him, "no. Sorry. You'll have to wait to see them. They're holding the press conference at the auditorium near the Mickey Mullen exhibit. He's here, you know."

"Imagine that," Benji said to the man. "Remind me to get his autograph . . . on a roll of toilet paper."

The man frowned. "You two going in or not?"

"We got these passes," Josh said, taking his out of his pocket. "We're playing in the tournament. Can you let us in and give us, like, a rain check so we can come back to see the rest of it?"

"Sorry," the man said. "One time only. I'd like to, but those are the rules."

"Maybe we can get some more of these," Josh said to Benji.

"Yeah," Benji said, slapping his pass down for the ticket man, "let's go."

Inside, a woman in a red skirt and white blouse with her back to them hooked up a velvet rope to block the doorway that led into the part of the exhibition where the press had gone. Josh looked around at the balls, bats, pennants, pictures, uniforms behind glass, and bronze statues from all the most famous players and teams the game had ever seen. He took a deep breath and let it out slowly.

"Benji," Josh said softly, "if Jaden can go in there with all those other people, I just can't see the harm if we slid in there too. This place is all about realizing your dreams, right?"

"Yeah, but I'm not dreaming of a jail cell," Benji said.

"Come on," Josh said, eyeing the red velvet ropes and the woman guarding them. "No one's gonna put two kids angling to see their heroes' statues behind bars."

"I don't know," Benji said, wrinkling his brow. "She's standing right there. I don't see how the heck we're gonna get past her."

"Shh," Josh said. "I got a plan. Follow me and don't say anything."

CHAPTER SIXTEEN

JOSH TOOK ONE STEP, then started to jog toward the woman and the red velvet rope. He waved his arms frantically and said, "Lady, lady, that guy in the ticket booth—I think he needs help!"

The woman spun around.

"He collapsed or something," Josh said, his voice filled with fake panic, "the guy with the glasses."

"Yeah," Benji said, pointing back toward the entrance. "His face turned all purple and he keeled over. Hurry!"

The woman's eyes went wide and her mouth became an O. She took off, running with her high heels clacking along the floor. Josh took Benji's arm, stepped over the rope, and tugged him along.

"Man, Josh," Benji said in an urgent whisper. "This is *great*."

"His face turned *purple*?" Josh said. "Jeez, Benji."

"You know I got a flair for the dramatic," Benji said. "Did you see her take off?"

"Come on," Josh said, "let's get out of here before she figures it out."

They rounded a corner and heard someone talking over a loudspeaker in a large hall, then a flurry of applause. They hurried past the crowd that stood watching the people up on a small stage at the end of the large space and soon lost their way in a deeper maze of empty passageways, displays, and small rooms. They walked quietly in the stillness and spoke in hushed voices so they could listen for the coming footsteps of the lady by the rope—just in case she decided to pursue them—or maybe something worse, like security guards.

"Man," Benji said after a while in a regular voice, "where's the Babe?"

"I think we just passed this way," Josh said, keeping his voice down. "There's Ty Cobb's cleats again."

"Yeah, imagine those things coming at you full speed," Benji said, loudly now. "They'd punch a hole in your lung if he hit you right. But we gotta find *the Babe*."

"Well, keep it down. We can't ask anyone now. That's for sure. Come on," Josh said, checking his watch and doing his best to enjoy the sights and ignore the feeling of dread that crept into his bones whenever he did something he knew he shouldn't really be doing.

They wandered some more and ended up right back at Ty Cobb's cleats.

"You got to be kidding me," Benji said, stamping around a couple more bends too quickly to look at anything before they stopped again.

That's when they heard someone coming.

CHAPTER SEVENTEEN

JOSH DUCKED BETWEEN A large glass display on the evolution of the catcher's mitt and the brick wall behind it, crouching low beside the wooden base and worming his way deeper in to make room for Benji, whose eyes had grown as large as grapefruits.

The voices kept coming. Benji gripped Josh's arm and froze.

"What are they gonna do to us, right?" Josh whispered hopefully into Benji's ear.

Benji's grip tightened and he said, "Arrest us, that's what."

"For *what*?" Josh asked, his heart chilled.

"I don't know," Benji said with a quavering voice. "Trespassing or criminal mischief or something. Shh."

Josh held still and listened and soon realized that the one voice belonged to a boy no older than them.

"So this is it," the boy said, his footsteps stopping almost next to Josh and Benji's hiding place. "Sandy Koufax."

"Really? Not your dad?" a girl's voice asked. It had a slight southern lilt to it.

"He was the best," the boy said as if he hadn't heard her question, "but he wouldn't play on Rosh Hashanah no matter what. I mean, who does things like that anymore?"

"Hey," Benji said, wriggling free from their hiding place before Josh could stop him. "Jaden? What's up? Josh, come on out, man. It's just Jaden."

Josh felt his face go hot with embarrassment as he struggled to get free. When he did, he noticed the gray powder of dust covering Benji's dark hair and shoulders. He looked down at his own clothes and realized he too was covered in dust.

"So, who's that?" Benji asked, pointing at the boy.

"Hi," the boy said, extending a hand to Benji, "I'm Mickey Mullen."

Josh knew his name before he said it. Mickey Mullen Jr. had wheat blond hair like his father, only curly. His skin was tan and his eyes pale blue. The smooth skin on his face reminded Josh of a statue he'd seen in an advertisement: Michelangelo's statue *David*. Josh touched the scar on his own discolored face.

Mickey wasn't as thick as Josh, but he stood just as tall, and he smiled sheepishly when Benji stared at his hand like it was a rotten fish.

Josh looked at Jaden, who scowled and said to Mickey, "Don't mind Lido; he wears his shirts so tight they cause a serious oxygen deficiency to the brain."

"What's that supposed to mean?" Benji asked, scowling right back and tugging on the collar of his T-shirt.

"I'm Josh," Josh said, shaking Mickey's hand and returning his smile. "She's right; don't mind him. He doesn't really mean it."

"This guy is the enemy," Benji said, raising his voice. "Are you two kidding me? Look at this guy—all that's missing is his surfboard."

Jaden stepped closer to Mickey and touched his hand. "Come on, Mickey. Thanks for showing me."

"What is he, like your new *boy*friend?" Benji said, pointing to Jaden's hand.

Jaden snatched her hand away from Mickey's and glared at Benji. "Easy, fathead."

"Now I'm a fathead?" Benji said, raising his voice to a roar. "*You* turn traitor to the Titans and you cheat on Josh and that makes *me* a fathead?"

"I'm not cheating on anyone!" Jaden shouted. "Josh isn't my boyfriend. He doesn't even *like* me like that. We're just friends."

Josh sighed and covered his face with one hand as he shook his head. Then he heard a sound that made him even sicker.

"There they are!" the woman from the velvet rope shouted. She nudged the security guards who accompanied her. "Those two right there!"

CHAPTER EIGHTEEN

ONE GUARD'S HAND BIT into Josh's shoulder while the other one's clamped down on Benji.

"Let's go," Josh's guard said in a low, rough voice.

Josh hung his head and let the man steer him toward the woman, but Benji resisted.

"Take your hands off me," Benji said, struggling free from the second guard. "I'll sue you if you touch me again. My mom's sister's husband works at a law firm."

"You can call your parents from the director's office," the woman said. "They can come get you after I fill them in on how you snuck in here."

"Oh man," Josh said, groaning. "Couldn't you just call the police?"

The woman gave him a funny look, then turned on

her heels and clacked away. Josh glanced back at Jaden, who stood beside Mickey Jr. with a look of shock and worry on her face. Mickey Jr. seemed unfazed. From above, the picture of Sandy Koufax seemed to scowl down at Josh, disappointed in a young ballplayer who didn't know enough to stay out of trouble.

Inside the director's office, Josh and Benji sat in two wooden chairs facing a big empty desk. On a table in front of a wall of bookshelves stood two magnificent trophies. Several people popped their heads inside the doorway to look them over before disappearing. The man from the ticket booth did the same thing, pausing long enough to cluck his tongue before shaking his head like the others and disappearing.

"Great idea," Benji said, his face buried in his hands. "My dad's gonna kill me if he has to come all the way here to get me. Man, I didn't even get to see the Babe's statue. Talk about exponential injustice."

"What's that?" Josh asked.

"I don't know," Benji said without removing his face from his hands. "I made it up. I heard Jaden use that word one time. I make stuff up when I'm depressed. Pretend I'm smart. Makes me feel better."

Josh sighed again. The knot in his stomach tightened when the woman reappeared with a white-haired man in a gray suit, who sat down at his desk.

"These are the boys, Ms. Simmons?" the director asked.

"They tried to ruin my event," she said, pursing her lips and nodding sharply. "They lied to me and they snuck in. Mr. Mullen was very precise that he wanted a press conference that was *closed* to the public. They embarrassed us all, and as the Mullens' official Cooperstown event planner, I want them banned from this place for life."

The director narrowed his eyes, then shook his head with a sigh. "I can't see banning two kids from the Hall of Fame for life, Ms. Simmons. This isn't a movie set, and that's not how we operate."

"At a minimum," she said, scowling at the director, "their parents need to make sure they stay away from Mr. Mullen for the rest of the week. I have several events planned, and I don't want these little stalkers showing up everywhere I turn."

Josh appealed to the director. "We just wanted to get our pictures with the statues of Hammering Hank and the Babe."

The director sighed and picked up his phone. "You want to give me your parents' number, son?"

Josh considered lying but thought about Sandy Koufax's scowling face and knew he'd only dig himself deeper. If this went on much longer he'd miss dinner, and his dad would come looking for him anyway and that would only make it worse. He said his father's number and the director began to dial.

"Wait," someone said.

Josh turned his head toward the doorway.

CHAPTER NINETEEN

"MR. MULLEN," THE WOMAN said.

The director put the phone back.

In the doorway, looking remarkably small next to his twelve-year-old son, stood Mickey Mullen. His craggy face was deeply tanned, and his dirty blond hair fell in shaggy waves nearly into his striking bottle-blue eyes. He smiled with perfect teeth as white and gleaming as the stretch limo that got Jaden. The muscles in his arms looked tight beneath a short-sleeved white polo shirt. On his wrist hung a gold watch big enough to belong in Josh's dad's toolbox at home, and his finger-nails had been carefully cut and polished to reflect the light.

When Mickey Mullen stepped into the room, Josh felt a current of excitement rush through his body. This was the man he'd seen in old sports clips and more recently on the big screen with nerves and fists of steel, defeating villains, and always ready to flash his knowing smile or crack a joke even in the face of serious danger. Josh felt like he knew Mickey Mullen, like Mickey Mullen was part of his life. Then he realized that Mickey didn't know him from twenty million other kids. Josh choked with a flush of words he wanted to use to impress the famous man, to show him all the ways in which he and Josh were exactly alike.

Mickey Mullen stepped into the room as if it were a stage and delivered his lines.

"You're our event planner for the week, right? Felicity, right?" Mickey Mullen said. "I think that means 'beautiful.'"

Felicity blushed. "Actually it means 'happy.'"

"Which is the same thing, isn't it?" Mickey Mullen said with a grin he now showed the director. "These boys are my son's new friends."

Mickey Mullen nodded toward Mickey Jr., who stood now in the doorway. When Jaden peeked around him to give Josh a thumbs-up, he knew that bringing Mickey in to save them had been her idea.

"I think this whole thing is just a misunderstanding," Mickey said. "Heck, it was my shindig, and I don't care that they got in."

"But Mr. Mullen, you said—"

Mickey Mullen smiled that smile and the woman froze, blinking just once before melting into a soft puddle of good humor.

Mickey turned to Josh, pointed at his cheek, and said, "Ouch. Hope you got the license plate of that truck."

"What truck?" Josh asked, baffled.

"The one that ran over your face," Mickey Mullen said, then laughed. "Only kidding, son, but what happened to you?"

"He got hit by a beanball," Benji said, breaking in on the conversation.

Josh scowled at Benji for answering the question that belonged to him.

"Sure," Mickey Mullen said. "Threw a couple beanballs myself back in the day. Part of the game, right, son?"

Josh didn't know what to say, so he touched his healing face, nodded lamely, and said, "I'm here for the tournament."

"I bet you are," Mickey Mullen said, turning to the two elaborate trophies and pointing to the slightly smaller one. "And I wish you all the best on the runner-up's trophy here. That's what this is, right?"

Mickey stepped to the table by the books and pointed to the smaller of the two trophies.

"Yes it is," the director said.

Josh knit his eyebrows. He couldn't keep from saying, "I play for the Titans, and we're planning to win the big one."

Mickey Mullen smiled at Josh with twinkling eyes and shook his head ever so slightly, as if that just wasn't going to happen. "Talk is cheap, and champions are like blue moons. They don't come around much."

"Mr. Mullen," Felicity said, "the director was just about to call these boys' parents."

"I've got a better idea," Mickey said. "I know just what these kids need."

CHAPTER TWENTY

JOSH AND BENJI LEANED back, afraid of what Mickey Mullen would say.

"An ice cream," Mickey Mullen said, breaking out into his big grin again. "That's what they need. These are *good* kids."

"Thank you, Mr. Mullen," Josh said, hearing the words leave his mouth like he was playing a role in a Mickey Mullen movie.

"Call me the Mick," the great man said with his smile burning bright. "That's what my friends call me. And watch out for those beanballs, will you?"

Before anyone could say another word, Benji jumped out of his seat, snatched a Sharpie marker from the director's desk, and handed it to Mickey Mullen along with his Red Sox cap. The star player signed it without looking, bumped fists with Benji and Josh, then blew a little kiss to the event planner before turning and leaving the room without another word.

"How cool was that?" Benji asked, examining the cap.

"You said toilet paper," Josh said. "I didn't think you liked Mickey Mullen."

"I'm not crazy about the guy," Benji said, "but he did play for the Red Sox, and this thing will be worth money."

"Boys," the director said, reaching into his desk, "here. Take these. Some extra passes. Come back as much as you like. I'm a Hank Aaron fan too."

"Thanks, mister," Josh said, accepting the passes and splitting them with Benji.

"Yeah, cool," Benji said. "Thanks."

"Come on," Josh said, tugging Benji toward the entrance. "They're all leaving."

Mickey Jr. and Jaden made up only the tail end of an entourage of people buzzing around Mickey Mullen, talking on cell phones, taking orders from him, or clearing the way. Cameras flashed when he emerged into the gray, wet day, ducked beneath an umbrella, and scooted inside a waiting limo.

An olive-skinned man with curly black hair, thick eyebrows, long sideburns, and a scowl emerged from the crowd and put his hand on Mickey Jr.'s shoulder. The man reminded Josh of an ape, despite his black suit and tie. His hunched-over frame rested on bow legs, and dark hair covered the backs of hands that hung like meat hooks.

While the man bent his mouth to Mickey Jr.'s ear, his black eyes scanned Josh and his friends.

"Your father is heading down to New York for dinner with Robert De Niro to talk about a new film," the man said, loud enough for them all to hear. "Did you decide if you're joining or going back to the hotel with the team? It's up to you."

"Well," Mickey Jr. said, looking sadly at his father's car as it pulled away from the curb without him. "I guess I'll go to the hotel. Hey, Myron? Can I give my friends a ride back to where they're staying first?"

The man called Myron looked them over and even cocked his head like a monkey before he said, "Well, we've got cars for the press. I'm sure we can squeeze them in somewhere and drop them."

"No," Mickey Jr. said, "I mean *my* car."

"Well, I've already got the coaches going in your car if you're headed back to the hotel," the man said, obviously put out.

Mickey Jr. shrugged and took a cell phone out of his jeans pocket.

"What are you doing?" the man asked.

"I'll give my dad a call and see if he can get me a car."

"Mickey, cut that out," the man said, swatting at the

phone with a hairy hand. "You know I give you whatever you want—I was just saying. Go ahead. Take your friends. The coaches can ride with me in my Town Car, and I'll just send the driver back for Glenda and Missy."

The man even held the limo door for them before closing it and slapping his hand on the roof to let the driver know he was set to go. The dark car—a shorter version of the one that had stopped for Jaden—eased out onto the street through a crowd of people who'd come out in the rain, hoping to catch a glimpse of Mickey Mullen.

"Who's Glenda and Missy?" Jaden asked, her notebook in hand.

"Oh," Mickey Jr. said, waving his hand, "just my father's stylist and makeup artist. Don't worry, they won't mind."

"Dude," Benji said, "your dad wears makeup?"

Jaden elbowed Benji in the ribs and he gulped.

"For movies and when he's on TV," Mickey Jr. said, grinning. "You know, a press conference like today or an interview or something. That's Hollywood."

"That's where you live?" Benji asked.

"Naw, Bel Air," Mickey Jr. said. "It's okay, I guess. Doesn't rain much, though. I kind of like rain. You know, how it cleans everything and all that."

"Well, welcome to upstate New York," Benji said, pointing his thumb out the window at the downpour. "Can't get much cleaner than this place. Who was the apeman?"

"Myron Underwood?" Mickey Jr. said. "He used to be my dad's bodyguard. Now he's kind of like a personal assistant."

"Assistant to what?" Benji asked.

Mickey Jr. shrugged. "My dad, I guess. He does all kinds of things and he's got, like, some tenth-degree black belt in jujitsu. What he really wants is a role in one of my dad's movies. He takes acting lessons."

"I bet the guy could get a part in *Planet of the Apes Two* pretty easy," Benji said.

Jaden elbowed Benji again.

"Thanks for saving us back there," Josh said. He sat on the bench seat riding sideways while Jaden sat between Benji and Mickey Jr. in the back.

"Jaden had the idea," Mickey Jr. said, "but I was happy to help."

"Dude," Benji said, "that lady was lucky she didn't call my dad. He would have given her something to think about. My dad plays football."

"Wow," Mickey Jr. said. "That's great. What team?"

"Oh, this semipro team where we live," Benji said proudly. "They don't get a ton of press, but last year they won the championship. I don't know, you might have read about that somewhere."

"That's cool," Mickey Jr. said.

"Lido," Jaden said, "this guy's dad won the World Series. Cut it out."

"Hey, he said it was cool," Benji said. "You heard

him. Football is a whole different sport. You don't just run around in a pair of knickers and socks when you play football. It's men only."

"Good grief," Jaden said, rolling her eyes. "I'm sorry for my friend here. He gets delirious if he doesn't get fed."

"I could use a hot dog if that's what you mean," Benji said.

"Just forget it," Jaden said, crossing her arms.

Josh tried to show her his smile to let her know Benji was just goofing around, but Jaden stared straight ahead for the rest of the ride out to the Beaver Valley Campsite. The only time anyone said anything was when they passed by Dream Park on their way out of town.

"There it is," Mickey Jr. said, touching the car window at the site of the enormous arched entryway to the sixteen fields. "I can't wait to get out there."

When they pulled into the gravel drive of the Beaver Valley Campsite, Josh's mom and dad were just walking up the path under an umbrella with Laurel wedged between them. They looked up with surprise at the limo.

"Hey, thanks a lot," Josh said.

"Yeah, thanks, dude, but don't expect me not to put it out of the park when we play you," Benji said, clicking his tongue twice against the roof of his mouth and winking at Mickey Jr. before slipping out of the car.

"No problem," Mickey Jr. said pleasantly. "You go get it, Lido."

Josh climbed out and waited for Jaden, who moved more slowly.

"So, Jaden," Mickey Jr. said softly to her. "If you give me your number, maybe we could, you know, get together or something this week sometime."

Josh bit into his lip.

CHAPTER TWENTY-ONE

JADEN GAVE HER CELL phone number to Mickey Jr., then repeated it before climbing out. Josh turned and started up the drive for the dining hall, where his parents waited on the porch.

"Josh," Jaden called, but he pretended he didn't hear.

"Hey," Benji said as the gravel crunched beneath the limo rolling off down the drive. "You know what I was thinking? What about the ice cream?"

"What ice cream?" Josh asked.

"The Mick," Benji said. "The Mick said he knew what we needed. What was that? Just some movie line? Crap."

"Go get some franks and beans, Lido," Jaden said, marching past. "God forbid you run low on gas."

Benji stopped in his tracks and Josh bumped into him.

"What's up with her?" Benji asked.

"Who cares," Josh said. "Let her new boyfriend deal with it."

Benji's eyes went wide. He looked from Josh to Jaden, then back to Josh, grinning. "Oh yeah. I *knew* it! And you are fuming, right?"

"I couldn't care less," Josh said, watching Jaden kiss her father's cheek as he met her on the path and they started toward the dining hall together.

"I don't know," Benji said doubtfully.

"Come on," Josh said, heading for the dining hall himself so he'd beat Jaden there. "Maybe we can get you some ice cream."

Benji bounced along beside him. "I want the Mick's ice cream so I can tell people, like, 'Hey, yeah, the Mick bought me this ice cream one time.' You know, so it wasn't just like I saw the guy. More like we hung out a little. Don't think I'm not reminding him about what he said when we play those guys, 'cause I will."

"We have to beat everyone else first," Josh said as they climbed the steps.

"We'll cream everyone else," Benji said. "Cream, like ice cream. Ha. Get it?"

"Get what?" Josh's dad asked.

"We met Mickey Mullen," Josh said.

"*The* Mickey Mullen?" his mom asked. "Not the son?"

"No, the real deal," Josh said.

"How exciting," his mom said.

"Yeah, people were going crazy," Josh said, then noticed the look on his father's face. "He's not that big, though, Mickey. Dad's, like, twice the size he is. Dad's the one who should be in those action movies. The actors they get to play the bad guys must be midgets, I swear."

"Not me," his dad said. "Tried out for *West Side Story* in middle school and it wasn't pretty."

Josh forced out a laugh, and it sounded like his mom did the same thing.

"The Mick owes me an *ice* cream," Benji said to Josh's mom before turning to his dad. "And don't worry, Coach. Mickey Mullen *and* his son both know that I can't be bribed out of being your heavy hitter and doing serious damage to their defense. Not for ice cream, any-way. Money might be another story, but no one's offered me any money. Yet."

"Way to go, Lido," Josh's dad said without much enthusiasm. "You're a true team player. Now, let's eat."

"Josh," his mom said as they sat down on one end of a long table amid the noise and mayhem of more than a hundred people passing along platters of hot dogs, hamburgers, buns and rolls, beans, and potato salad, "there's Jaden and Dr. Neidermeyer. You should invite them to sit with us."

"No, that's all right, Mom," Josh said, taking two dogs.

"Joshua," his mom said as she passed the rolls. "I'd

like to be able to ask you to have good manners, but I'll tell you if that's what it takes. She's your friend and she came all this way to write about you and your father's team. The least you can do is be polite."

Josh clenched his teeth.

"She's doing a lot more than writing about Josh," Benji said, slathering a dog with ketchup and stuffing half of it into his mouth.

Josh's mom took a dollop of potato salad as she gave Benji a questioning look, but the only thing that got past his hot dog chomping was a silly grin. She turned her eyes on Josh.

"Her editor asked her to do a story about Mickey Mullen is all," Josh said. "We just don't want to hear about it anymore."

"That's no reason not to be polite," his mom said.

"Look," Josh said, pointing to Jaden and her father as they sat down at another table next to the Eschelmans. "She's fine. She knows half the team, Mom."

His mom opened her mouth to say something, but his father put a hand on her arm.

"Laura," he said, nodding to the plate of hamburgers, "let's get those burgers going and let the boys start thinking about baseball instead of girls and action movies, okay?"

Josh's mom studied his dad for a moment, then swept a strand of hair behind her ear, and said, "That's a good idea. Let's eat."

Josh watched Jaden from the corner of his eye as he

pretended to listen to Benji telling a story about how his father once ate two dozen hot dogs in a contest.

"He must have gotten quite sick," Josh's mom said.

"Oh yeah," Benji said, "you should have seen it, chunks everywhere. Our dog, Bingo, didn't care, though. He went right after them. Joke was on him, though, 'cause next thing you know, Bingo starts puking. Bad thing was that he gets it on my leg and the smell gets me gagging and next thing you know, *I* puke. Basically a puke fest."

Josh's mom set her burger down, cleared her throat, wiped her mouth on a napkin, and said, "So, let's talk about baseball. I know there are, like, thirty-two teams here and you need to win four rounds to get into the finals, but who do you guys play in the first round? When do you face the Comets?"

"The first round is a team from Miami," Josh's dad said through a mouthful of food. "The Barracudas. The brackets got drawn randomly. We're in the upper bracket with fifteen other teams, and the Comets are in the lower bracket. The only way we'll face them is if we both make it to the championship game, the finals."

"Five games in all?" Josh's mom said. "How come we're here for eight days?"

"They need extra time in case we get rained out," his father said. "If the weather looks good, they'll just have a day or two where they can spread out the schedule a bit, let some of the teams rest up. That'll all be the luck of the draw, too."

"First round ought to be a breeze, right, Coach?" Benji said. "Our real rivals are the Comets, right?"

Josh's dad swallowed, shook his head, and said, "You don't know who your real rival is until you play them. A rival is a team that's just as good as you are, maybe even a little better, but a team you play your very best against."

"But we only play teams here once," Benji said.

"But you know by how that goes that you're going to be seeing the team, or maybe just some of the players, somewhere down the line," Josh's dad said. "And the team from Florida? Don't take them lightly. They play more baseball in Florida than anywhere. The kids we play will be faster, more skillful, and more experienced, especially on defense, than any we've seen before."

"So," Benji said, a look of confusion on his face, "we can't win this? I thought we were one of the favorites to win. Us and the Comets."

"I didn't say we couldn't win," Josh's dad said. "I just said that overall, the Florida players might be even better than ours."

"So how do we win if they're better?" Benji asked.

Josh's dad winked at Josh and Benji and said, "You don't have to *be* better—you just have to *play* better."

CHAPTER TWENTY-TWO

SUNSHINE WASHED OVER THE fields at Dream Park as the opening day of the tournament began. The sound of bats clanging and crowds cheering mixed with the smells of fresh grass, baking dirt, and food grilling. The day for Josh didn't begin so well. Seeing Mickey Jr. in the parking lot surrounded by a crowd eager to have their pictures taken with him left Josh's mind wandering. And in spite of a successful week of hitting the ball in practice, his mask felt uncomfortable. He shifted it about between pitches during his first at bat, and the loss of focus helped him to strike out. After his teammates began to connect, though, he left the mask alone and found his groove, driving two over the fence.

Only a slight breeze stirred. The air and the lush grass grew steadily warmer as morning crept toward noon. The Barracudas maintained their lead, and Josh thought more and more about his father's words of warning the night before.

While the Barracuda pitcher wasn't up to the standard of Sandy Planczeck, the players around him were demons in the field, snatching up fly balls, scooping grounders, and making throws as quick and easy as sneezing. The Barracudas could hit, too, and in the top of the sixth, with three men on base, it took a solo double play from Josh, snagging a wicked line drive and tagging the runner on second before he could get back to the base, to put down the side. The Titans were still in it, only down 5–4.

Esch began the bottom of the sixth with a single, and Josh followed with a double that sent Esch home for the tying run. The next two batters went down swinging, leaving the Titans' survival in Benji's hands. That's when Josh's dad gave him the signal to steal after the second pitch. Josh stood on second like a potted plant, and the pitcher threw a high ball that Benji swung at anyway. Josh never even moved.

But on the next pitch, he took off.

The catcher got caught slacking and made the throw late, with Josh burning up the baseline and sliding safe into third. He bounced up and slapped the dirt off his pants, his heart racing at the signal from his dad to steal if it was there. To Josh, that meant even the slightest fumble by the catcher and he would go. Benji hadn't gotten on base yet, and—as unlikely as it was to safely steal home—Josh's dad was betting on Josh's speed over Benji's bat. This time, though, the Barracudas wouldn't be caught unaware.

Benji did his best, swinging at a curveball and missing, then missing on a changeup. Neither pitch left Josh an opening. Both times the ball smacked soundly into the catcher's mitt with the catcher popping straight up to stare Josh down with the ball cocked back, ready to throw.

Josh's dad tipped his hat and tugged his earlobe before tapping two fingers on his arm and then giving a series of fake signals. The initial signal, emphasized by the two fingers on his arm, meant steal home no matter what. When the ball crossed the plate, Josh would take off.

Josh took a deep breath, dug his cleats into the dirt at the base of the bag, and prayed for a ball.

CHAPTER TWENTY-THREE

THE PITCHER WOUND UP and let one fly. Josh timed it so that he took off as the ball crossed the plate, running all out at a blazing speed.

The pitch went wide of the plate. The catcher dove and Josh felt a surge of delight. But as the catcher rolled in the dirt, he twisted and sprang to his feet with the ball in hand. He'd made a spectacular save. Josh envisioned plowing over the catcher—the ball spilling from his glove—for the big win.

But as he neared the plate, he realized that this catcher was smarter than that. Instead of waiting down the line, he'd planted himself firmly over the plate, extending the ball, pinned into his mitt with his right hand. Without a body to knock down, Josh didn't stand a chance of running him over before he'd been tagged out. He made that calculation in a split second, stopped, and raced back for third, thinking Benji might be able to get a hit after all.

Three-quarters of the way back, he sensed the catcher's throw zip past his ear and saw the ball land in the third baseman's glove. Josh reversed field again, sprinting for home. When something cracked into the back of his helmet, he grinned. The third baseman threw wild and the ball ricocheted off Josh's helmet toward the mound. He dug in, churning forward, aware of the pitcher scooping up the ball and the catcher back in the perfect position at home.

Everyone shouted. Josh somehow sensed the catcher adjusting his glove for the throw. Josh stumbled and dove, headfirst. He heard the smack of the ball into the catcher's mitt, but his fingers touched the bag just below it before the tag came.

"Safe!" the umpire yelled.

The Titans went wild.

After a lot of backslapping and cheering among his teammates, Josh lined up to shake hands with the Florida kids along with everyone else. Then the team circled up around his dad.

"Okay, nice win, you guys. Esch, way to get on base with that single. LeBlanc, way to close the deal," his dad said, all business, looking down and flipping through the pages on his clipboard. "So, we advance, but we still have a long way to go—three more wins to make it to the championship—so let's not celebrate too hard here. Tomorrow we'll play the winner of the Nashville Roadsters and the Toronto Eagles in the second round."

"Roadsters?" Benji said, raising one eyebrow. "What's that? A car or a barnyard animal?"

Josh's dad looked at Benji and said, "They're twenty-three and one so far this season, so it doesn't matter what they are, right?"

"Right, Coach," Benji said, coming to attention and saluting.

When Josh's dad cracked a smile, the rest of the team laughed.

"The Roadsters and the Eagles play in about an hour, one o'clock on field seven," his dad said, "so you guys get a bite to eat and let's meet over there to scout things out."

The team put their hands in, did a chant, and broke up. Jaden waited beside the backstop with her pad and paper. Josh wandered over, expecting Jaden to praise their performance, kicking up dust with his cleat and studying the ground.

"Hey," he said. "We're going to scout the next team we play. You up for it?"

"Oh, hi, Josh," Jaden said, looking up as if she hadn't seen him. "Nice steal at home. Exciting finish."

"You writing about that?" Josh asked, craning his neck to see her pad.

Jaden snapped the pad shut and forced a smile.

"They'll let me run a paragraph. Maybe two. It's only the first round. Long way to go."

"Yeah," Josh said, nodding. "So. What about going with us to scout? I'll buy you a hot dog or something."

"No thanks," Jaden said, picking up the backpack she'd set on the edge of the bleachers.

"A soda or something?" he asked.

"I gotta go over to field eleven," she said, looking at her watch. "Get some follow-up stuff for my story on Mickey."

"Junior or senior?" Josh asked.

Jaden stared at him with those green cat eyes, and the yellow flecks seemed to swirl, almost hypnotizing him. "Does it matter, Josh?"

Anger erupted inside Josh like lava busting out the side of a volcano.

"No," he said, "it doesn't. You want to know why?"

"Tell me," Jaden said, sounding bored.

"Because who cares about some Hollywood actor who used to play baseball? Who cares about his stuck-up kid?" Josh asked, raising his voice.

Jaden raised her chin. "He is *not* stuck up. He's very nice, and he helped save your butt yesterday, you and that goofy friend of yours. You guys could hardly thank him."

"Last thing I knew, Benji was your friend too, but obviously old friends don't matter to you when some movie actor and his kid show up," Josh said.

"Someone calling for a heavy hitter?" Benji said, popping out from around the corner of the dugout. "I heard my name."

"Stash it," Jaden said to him.

"Stow it," Josh said.

"Lovers' quarrel, I guess," Benji said, disappearing.

"Those guys sure didn't do anything for *me*," Josh said. "If anything, they did it for you so you would write good things about them. That's all those two are worried about—flying people around to write good things. Don't kid yourself. Those people don't care about anything but themselves."

"You should know about that," Jaden said, turning to go.

CHAPTER TWENTY-FOUR

JOSH AND BENJI HELPED Josh's dad take the gear to the bus, then they headed to field seven. The winner of the game being played there would be their next opponent. With his mind on trying to get things back to normal with Jaden, Josh had a hard time focusing on the action in front of him. Halfway through the game, Benji nudged Josh in the ribs and he jumped, spilling his nachos all over his dad's lap.

"Josh, what the heck?" his father said, wiping a smear of melted cheese from his knee.

"Sorry, Dad," Josh said.

His father's face softened and he pointed at the field. "How about this Chase Corcoran from Toronto? Kid can throw. He's just closing out the last two innings, so we'll see him in our game. I know I said I'd give you guys the rest of the day off, but I think I'd like to get some batting practice in later. You see that slider?"

"Slider?" Josh said, looking out at the lanky pitcher on the mound.

"You even watching?" his dad asked.

Josh felt his face heat up. "Sure."

"Right," his dad said.

"Well," Josh said, scratching the back of his neck. "I know—like you said—that we've got three more games to win before the championship, but I just keep thinking about the Comets playing over there on field eleven.

"Would you mind if I went over there?"

His father looked at him with mild surprise and said, "You're taking this rival thing serious, huh?"

"Kind of."

Josh's dad broke out in a grin and he nodded. "Yeah, I get it. You go ahead. I can handle the scouting here by myself."

Josh left the bleachers just as Corcoran struck out his third batter in a row. Benji hustled along beside him and said, "I'm all for seeing the Comets, but we ought to make a pit stop."

Benji pointed toward the concession stand, but Josh didn't stop his quick march or say anything until he stood there at the corner of the bleachers at field eleven.

"What the heck?" Josh said, his head swiveling this way and that, all around. "I don't even see her."

"Her? Who?" Benji said, wrinkling his forehead. "Jaden?"

"Who do you think?" Josh said, still scanning.

"Dude, you are so in love," Benji said. "I thought we were here to scout these Comet guys. Hey, would you look at all those cameras and reporters? We had Jaden taking some crummy notes, but for these guys it's like they're shooting a movie or something."

"Right, all the reporters, but no Jaden," Josh said. He sighed angrily, still searching the stands and anyone within eyesight of field eleven. "Something's not right."

"Right or not," Benji said. "We should at least watch a little."

"Okay," Josh said, starting to climb the crowded bleacher steps even as he continued to search. "Let's sit down."

They sat and watched the game for half an inning before Benji nudged Josh again and said, "Hey! Look! There she is."

CHAPTER TWENTY-FIVE

JADEN SAT IN THE dugout between Mickey Mullen and Mickey Mullen Jr., wearing a bright red Comets cap and clutching her notepad. Her smile seemed to glow.

"You've got to be kidding me," Josh said. "*A Comets hat?*"

"Women," Benji said, shaking his head. "Can't live with 'em, can't live without 'em."

Josh gave him a dirty look.

"Come on," Benji said. "My dad says that all the time. I'm sorry. Let's just go."

"No, that's fine," Josh said. "Let's scout these chumps."

"Look, I know you don't want to sit here looking at Jaden sandwiched between those two guys," Benji said.

"I couldn't care less," Josh said. "Just be quiet and watch some baseball, Benji. Think about the game a little more, will you?"

Josh forced himself not to look at Jaden, a feat that became much easier when the inning closed out and Mickey Mullen Jr. took the mound against the Tallahassee Knights. Josh studied his rival, watching carefully the windup and delivery that was as unique to every pitcher as his signature. Mullen moved with long, sweeping motions, releasing the ball with a final snap of the wrist that took advantage of his long arms and maximized the velocity of the ball. The kid could throw, and not just fastballs. His only issue seemed to be accuracy, and the tall, skinny umpire took care of that. In fact, the umpire's apparent strike zone was so high and so wide that Josh found himself studying the man's pinched and narrow face as he lifted his mask to take a drink of water between innings.

The ump had a long nose, flattened to his face, and an unending scowl. When he walked, he swung one leg with a distinctive limp. Part of the scowl, Josh thought, might have been to deflect the constant complaints from the Tallahassee coach, who groaned loudly and shouted protests over the liberal strike zone.

The game moved into the top of the final inning with the score tied at two. Mickey Mullen Jr. hit a double, sending the runner on second home and giving the Comets the lead before the Tallahassee pitcher put down three batters in a row, closing out the side. With a 3–2 lead, Mickey Jr. took the mound again. The Mick emerged from the dugout and urged on the crowd, waving his arms with the drama of a symphony conductor. The crowd stood and cheered, wild for the movie star.

The Mick then made a gallant gesture with his arm toward the pitcher's mound and bowed to his son. The crowd ate up the theatrics, and a storm of applause rained down on Mickey Jr. Even after the noise had settled to a steady cheer, excitement buzzed in the air, and Josh couldn't help wondering what it would be like to have a dad that famous. He stole a glance at Jaden. She stood too, inside the dugout, clapping her hands with the rest of them.

"Half the time the guy can't get it over the plate," Josh said with disgust, leaning into Benji's ear, "and they're clapping like he's Roger Clemens."

Benji did his best to make farting noises by blowing on his arm, but it was no use. All eyes were on the Mick, his glowing eyes, his shining teeth, and his all-star son on the mound. The thrill must have gotten to Mickey Jr. because his first three pitches were so wild, the catcher had to come out of his stance to snag them. The ump correctly called all three balls. Finally Mickey Jr. put one down the middle, but it passed the batter at eye level.

"Strike!" the ump called, pumping his fist.

"What?" the Tallahassee coach screamed. "Are you

crazy? That ball was almost over his head."

The ump ignored the coach and crouched down behind the plate.

"You've got to be *kidding* me, Ump!" the Tallahassee coach screamed.

Josh studied Jaden. It looked like she was sitting a little more rigid than she had been a few minutes ago. The next pitch came waist high but outside, a close call.

"Strike!" the ump said.

The Tallahassee coach went berserk, running out onto the dirt. The umpire whipped off his mask and snarled at the coach.

"You get back in the dugout or you are *out* of here, Coach," the ump said. "Set an example for the kids, would you?"

"*You* set an example," the coach shouted. "I've never seen calls that bad."

"One more word, Coach, and you're done."

The Tallahassee coach stamped back to his dugout and began shouting encouragement to his team, but even though his words were positive, his anger came through loud and clear. The next pitch was inside. The batter hesitated and Josh knew what went through his mind—if it was even close, he might as well swing. He swung and missed.

The crowd cheered as if they'd forgotten the pathetic calls and so it went, with the next batter striking out on an 0–2 count. The third man up was the top of the Talla-hassee order. He surprised everyone by hunting for a high pitch and connecting, blasting a line drive over the first baseman's head. The next batter came out swinging, too, jumping at an outside pitch and connecting enough so that he dribbled one down the third-base line.

With two runners on, the next batter went hunting as well. It was obvious that the irate Tallahassee coach had told his best batters to swing at anything they could. Meanwhile Mickey Jr. seemed to suddenly gain control. The first pitch came inside fast, then broke out-side across the plate. The batter swung but missed. The next pitch was low, but he swung anyway, hitting it foul. For three more pitches in a row, the batter defended the plate, swinging at everything but delivering nothing except foul balls.

Finally, a ball came down the middle with heat.

The batter swung and connected, sending a red-hot grounder past the edge of the mound. The shortstop made a great play by diving and just getting a glove on the ball to slow it down. The runners took off. The cen-ter fielder ran in on the wounded grounder. The runner from second rounded third, and the third-base coach waved him home.

The center fielder scooped up the ball, one-hopped, and made the throw to home. The runner slid, kicking up a cloud of dirt as the umpire crouched nearby with his eyes glued to the plate. The runner's foot hit home plate just as the catcher stretched up and snagged the throw. The catcher brought his glove down and slapped the runner's leg, nearly a second too late.

"Out!" the umpire shouted, throwing a thumb over his right shoulder.

"Out?" the losing coach shrieked amid the cheering crowd.

"Tagged him before the foot touched the plate, Coach," the umpire shouted. "He's out."

"Out? He was *safe!*" the coach screamed, whipping off his hat and slapping it against his leg. "You're blind! You're a moron! You're a crook!"

The coach threw his hat down and stomped on it. Then he balled his hands into fists and ran right at the umpire.

CHAPTER TWENTY-SIX

THE COACHES FROM BOTH teams swarmed home plate, grappling with the head-coach-gone-crazy and fending him off the umpire. Mickey Mullen stood outside the Comets dugout with his arms crossed and grinning, shaking his head in disappointment at the madness but staying well away from the action. He turned to the crowd and offered up a dramatic shrug as if to say that some people were simply crazy. The umpire didn't back down. In fact, he went after the Tallahassee coach— who was being restrained—and nearly got a punch off before two of the Comets' assistant coaches got hold of him and dragged him away.

"Holy moly," Josh said.

"It's like a Syracuse Express football practice," Benji said, gawking. "Those guys are always going at it, only the coaches just let 'em fight 'cause they say they don't get paid enough to get a black eye."

"But did you see that call?" Josh said. "It was the worst call I've ever seen."

"Not the worst," Benji said. "Remember when we were in Philadelphia and that ump called it an out when the guy dropped the pop fly but scooped it up and put it in his glove but the ump couldn't see that far? *That* had to be the worst."

"Well, one of the worst then," Josh said. "That was awful."

"Yeah, well, that's what happens when your dad is in the movies," Benji said. "That ump is probably looking for tickets to the Oscars or something."

"Well, he earned them, I'll tell you," Josh said, shaking his head and slipping into the press of people exiting the bleachers.

"You gonna try and talk to Jaden?" Benji asked.

"Forget Jaden," Josh said, pulling out his phone. "I'm calling my dad."

But when Josh called his dad's cell phone, he learned that his dad had already left.

"Your mom asked me to get some grape juice at the store for your sister," his dad said, "but I'll come back and get you guys if you're ready."

"No," Josh said. "That's okay. You talked to the driver about us being banned from the shuttle bus?"

"She's all set," Josh's dad said in a low rumble that meant business. "I had a talk with the camp manager.

You guys can ride, but keep the comments to yourselves, right? Tell that to Benji, too."

Josh smiled to himself. "I will. So, we'll just catch the shuttle. Maybe we'll even take it into town and see the Babe's statue. Benji's dying to get a shot with it, and I want to see Hammerin' Hank's. Then we can take the shuttle home later."

"Don't miss dinner," his dad said. "I'm going to have batting practice right afterward. This Corcoran kid's got me worried."

"No problem, Dad."

Josh hung up and he and Benji made their way to the entrance, where they found the powder blue Beaver Valley Campsite shuttle bus just getting ready to leave. The driver glared at them as they climbed the steps, but several parents and players from the Titans were already on the bus, heading for town, and the driver seemed to consider them with a glance before she said anything nasty.

"No trouble," she said, growling under her breath with obvious hatred.

"We won't," Josh said.

"Trouble's what you make of it," Benji said, strutting by.

"Meathead," Josh said in a whisper as they took their seats, "what does that even mean?"

"Sounded good," Benji said. "Like a ninja or something."

"A ninja?"

"Or a Buddhist or something. I don't know. Just work with me."

"Like that umpire worked with the Comets?" Josh asked, shaking his head in disgust.

"You don't have to be as obvious as that," Benji said. "That guy's lucky the Comets fans outnumbered the Tallahassee people by about twenty to one or there might have been a riot."

"I mean, I've seen some bad calls," Josh said, "but that guy took it to a whole new level."

"Starstruck, I guess," Benji said. "You saw what the Mick did with that crowd. Like putty in his hands."

They got off the bus in the center of town with the rest of the crowd from the Beaver Valley Campsite. Josh and Benji fell in with a handful of their teammates who were also heading for the museum. They walked up Pioneer Alley, and at the corner of Main, where the turn for the museum was, Josh saw Mickey Jr.'s limo with its blacked-out windows heading their way. He grabbed Benji by the arm and pulled him aside.

"Look," he said, pointing.

"I told you, dude," Benji said, freeing his arm. "I'm not impressed with big cars."

"Not the car," Josh said, lowering his voice as the rest of the group kept going and the limo rolled past. "Jaden. You think she's in there?"

Benji wrinkled his nose. "Nah."

Then Benji said, "Maybe."

"Maybe?" Josh asked.

"They were sitting pretty close in that dugout."

"Thanks," Josh said, turning to go.

"You asked," Benji said. "Hey, where you going?"

"To see," Josh said, taking off at a jog as the limo continued on down Pioneer Alley toward the waterfront.

CHAPTER TWENTY-SEVEN

THE LIMO TURNED THE corner on Lake Street and Josh sped up. His breath was growing short by the time he reached Lake, so he was glad to see the limo make a left and turn into the marina. Visions of Jaden and Mickey Jr. going sailing together or taking a cruise in some antique boat with one of those comfy leather love seats in the back turned his stomach. By the time he rounded the corner and darted into the marina's long parking lot, the limo had already come to a stop down by the water.

Josh scanned the docks, which extended a couple hundred feet out into the lake with boats nosed into them on either side. There wasn't too much activity, and after a couple minutes his visions of a romantic boat ride were put to rest. Then his heart gave another lurch as he thought of the two of them, alone, sitting in the back of the limousine with the air-conditioning blowing cool and the music down low. He approached the long black car, but the engine appeared to be off and the driver had a newspaper out on the wheel, reading the sports section. He looked up as Josh strolled past, and Josh waved, peering all the way in through to the backseat.

It was empty.

Josh looked around for where they'd gone. Of the two long buildings facing each other across the parking lot, one was a motel and the other was for boat storage and repair. Then Josh spotted the restaurant.

He opened the door and peeked inside. Even in the middle of the afternoon, the tables overlooking the big windows were crowded and noisy. Colorful wooden fish hung from the ceiling, along with lamps shaped like anchors. Josh stepped in and scanned the room, seeing no sign of Jaden. He scanned the room again and was just turning to go when a head of dark curly hair caught his eye. The half of the face he could see sitting across from the person with the curly hair poked at his memory. He studied the high red cheek, small dark eye, and long flat nose of the pinched face.

The umpire from the Comets game.

For a better view of the other man, Josh circled along the bright blue wall, beneath a yellow, blue, and green dolphin fish and, beneath that, a table of old men whose straw hats shook with laughter. Then he saw the face of the curly-headed man.

Myron, the bodyguard in the black suit. He was grinning at the umpire and waving his hand in the air with a kingly expression. The two men exchanged a few words. Myron took a sip of coffee, then slipped the umpire a bulging manila envelope before he stood to go.

Staying a few paces back, Josh followed Myron toward the door. He had to worm his way through a handful of customers waiting to be seated to get to the glass. He peered through just in time to see Myron climb back inside his limousine and pull away.

When Josh turned around, he gasped and stumbled back against the door. The umpire stood there, staring at Josh with an angry scowl.

His hand reached out and Josh ducked.

CHAPTER TWENTY-EIGHT

"**GET OUTTA MY WAY,** kid," the umpire said, his hand snaking past Josh and pushing open the glass door. "No wonder you got hit in the face, standing around, blocking people's ways."

Josh touched the healing scar on his cheek, stepped aside, and followed the umpire with his eyes as he limped across the parking lot and climbed into a rusty red pickup truck. Josh headed for the road, his instincts telling him to follow the man as far as he could. When the red pickup reached the street, it went left. Josh took off after it, sprinting down the sidewalk as the truck slowly pulled away. At the end of the street, it turned right. Josh thought about giving up, knowing there was no way he could follow a truck on foot, but something told him to do his best.

He took off after the truck, and just as he reached the corner, his efforts were rewarded. He caught the flash of a yellow fender as the red truck disappeared into a driveway no more than two blocks up the street.

Josh trudged up River Street until he came to the spot where the truck had disappeared. Two small stone pillars marked the gravel drive that cut into the center of a woods. On one pillar, a black sign with fluorescent orange letters announced NO TRESPASSING. With a thumping heart, Josh crossed the street and dove into the underbrush, keeping the gravel drive in sight and staying parallel to its path in the web of tree trunks and dappled sunlight. He tried to walk quietly, but sticks and leaves snapped and rustled beneath his feet. He looked around. Other than the long gravel drive, he saw nothing except thick woods heavy with vines and brambles.

After a particularly nasty patch of thorns forced him deeper into the woods and out of sight of the gravel road, he found himself without a marker of any kind. He listened but heard only birds twittering and an airplane high overhead, which told him nothing. Hot frustration with a froth of fear bubbled up inside as he asked himself how he could get lost in a woods so close to the middle of a town. He turned and tried to retrace his steps to get back to the driveway, pushing through briars and thickets of close-knit saplings. Finally, the thick knot of vegetation opened into a cool wood of towering trees.

He crossed a gurgling stream and climbed its far bank. When he reached its lip, he saw something through the trees, rising up nearly above their tops.

As he drew closer, he began to use the trunks of massive trees for cover until he stood at the edge of an unkempt lawn, staring up at a weathered gray house with steep, pointy roofs, warped shutters, and gingerbread trim broken with rot. The back lawn of the old house sloped downward, and through the trees Josh saw the glint of sunlight on the river. The only sign of human life was the red pickup truck parked in front of a detached garage on the far side of the house.

Josh circled the house, darting from tree to tree. He passed beneath a porch that wrapped itself around the entire back of the house, then rounded the corner of the far side. He shivered when he saw a couple dozen crooked and crumbling gravestones poking their heads up from weedy beds in the side yard. When the back door swung open with a creak, Josh ducked for cover but peered out to see the umpire in a floppy pair of flowery swim trunks. On his face he wore dark sunglasses and a huge smile. Under his arm was a newspaper, a towel, and a bottle of suntan oil.

The umpire made his way down the hill toward an aging boathouse with a small dock jutting out into the water. When the umpire emerged from the boathouse carrying a gas can, Josh retreated to the front of the house, studying it for signs of life before taking off at a fast walk down the gravel driveway, happy to be getting out of there without having to trek back through the woods.

The long gravel drive wound through the woods, and the stone pillars had just come into sight when he heard the crunch of gravel behind him. Before he could react, the red truck appeared like something out of a bad dream, moving fast. It blared its horn. Josh jumped, stumbled, and fell directly in front of its path. The truck slid toward him in a spray of gravel and a swirl of dust.

CHAPTER TWENTY-NINE

WHEN JOSH OPENED HIS eyes, he saw the truck's steaming nose just inches from his face. The umpire appeared over him, shaking a bony finger.

"Are you crazy? I almost wrecked my truck!" the man said, screeching like a ghoul with wide bloodshot eyes, pointing at the steaming truck. "Who are you? You see that sign? You're trespassing!"

Josh scrambled to his feet. He froze for a moment, and the umpire reached to grab him. Josh turned and bolted.

The man hollered after him, but Josh never looked back. He hit the street and sprinted toward Main. When he got there, he glanced quickly over his shoulder, saw no one behind him, and ran straight for the Hall of Fame. He ran so hard that by the time he got there, he thought he'd be sick. In the alcove between the different wings of the building, he braced his hand on a bench and fell to a knee, breathing deep through his nose.

"Dude, where've you been?" Benji asked, poking Josh's shoulder. "I found the Babe. You gotta go back in with me. I swear, you can see a resemblance."

Josh looked up and squinted at Benji in the sunlight. "Resemblance to what?"

"Me," Benji said, holding up his cell phone. "Me and the Babe."

Josh took a deep breath and shook his head.

"I'm telling you," Benji said, holding forth the screen until Josh looked. "Hey, what's the matter?"

"I just saw a payoff, that's what," Josh said, rising to his feet and glancing around at the steady stream of visitors washing past them.

"Payoff for what?" Benji asked.

"Not so loud," Josh said, pressing a finger to his lips. He took Benji by the elbow and led him down the street, away from the crowd, and then told him what he'd seen—the meeting between the umpire and Myron, where the umpire had gone, the red truck, the gravestones in a small cemetery outside the house, and how Josh had almost been run over by the guy.

"What? The umpire *lives* here?" Benji asked, stopping at the corner in front of Carmen Esposito's Italian Ice Cream.

"Maybe," Josh said, moving aside for a family with

several small children who jingled a bell on the door as they stepped out onto the sidewalk from the ice-cream store, "but the truck had a Pennsylvania license plate. The ump acted like he owned the place, though, screaming about trespassing and all. It's a pretty creepy place, whatever it is, and I swear the guy looks like he crawled out of one of those graves in the side lawn."

"So the ump got paid to make those crappy calls?" Benji said, wrinkling his face in disgust. "That's incredible. How the heck can you win against that? How much was it?"

"I don't know," Josh said, shaking his head. "The envelope was pretty thick, and you can't compete with that. The calls that guy made today?"

"So," Benji said, "no way we can win this thing. Should we tell your dad?"

Josh thought for a minute, then shook his head. "No, he can't do anything."

"We just let them do it?" Benji said.

"No, *we* find out what's going on," Josh said. "Maybe we can take a picture of them meeting or something, Myron giving him the cash."

"You think they'll keep paying him?" Benji asked.

"I don't know," Josh said, "but it looked to me like the ump fixed the game this morning, then they paid him off. Maybe they hold back the money until he comes through. If so, we've got to catch them in the act. We'll get a copy of the schedule and just see when the Comets play next."

"But there are, like, eight games tomorrow, and that's just counting the teams that are still alive," Benji said, peering over Josh's shoulder into the big bay window of the ice-cream shop. "You think it'll be the same umpire?"

"I don't know," Josh said. "Maybe he's got that fixed too."

Benji wasn't listening; he was bobbing his head around to get a good look into the window.

"I know, Benji," Josh said with a sigh, "you need an ice cream."

"That's not what I'm looking at, dude," Benji said, pointing.

CHAPTER THIRTY

THE BELL ON THE door to the ice-cream shop jingled. Josh turned around and groaned when he saw who it was. Jaden had her arm hooked through Mickey Jr.'s arm, both of them eating ice-cream cones. She leaned over and licked Mickey Jr.'s mint chocolate chip cone and they laughed together. Her eyes went right past Josh.

Josh reached out and touched her arm as she walked by.

"Jaden," he said. "Can I talk to you?"

"Oh, hi, Josh," she said, acting as if she hadn't seen him. "Sure. What's up?"

"Alone?" Josh said, nodding at Mickey.

"I think that whatever you have to say, you can say in front of Mickey," Jaden said.

"Dude, you are so lame," Benji said to her. "After

everything we've done for you, this is how you act?"

"Let's see," Jaden said, glaring at Benji. "What have you done for me, Lido? You've teased me. You've insulted me. You've embarrassed me. Umm . . ."

"Josh needs to talk to you," Benji said. "That should be enough."

"You guys go ahead," Mickey said, holding up his cell phone. "I need to make a call anyway. I'll wait for you on that bench around the corner, Jaden."

"Mickey," Jaden said, "you don't have to—"

"No, that's okay," Mickey said. He gave her hand a pat and unhooked his arm. They watched him round the corner, eating chocolate sprinkles off his mint chocolate chip.

"Josh, loan me a five, will you?" Benji said. "I need a double-decker before we hit Doubleday Field. You want something too? I might need ten."

Josh fished ten dollars out of his pocket and handed it to Benji. He asked for three scoops of chocolate on a cone, the watched Benji disappear into the shop with a jingle of the bells.

"Can we walk?" Josh asked.

"Not far," she said, nodding toward where Mickey had gone. "I don't want to be rude."

"Jaden," Josh said. "I feel like all of a sudden we're not friends anymore and I don't even know exactly why."

"But you know partially why, right?" she said, licking her cone as they took slow steps down the shady side of the street.

"You act like you've known Mickey for years," Josh said. "You just met the guy. You have no idea what he's about."

"I have instincts," she said.

"Well, instinct this," Josh said, and he told her the story of what he'd seen, trying to read her face as she listened but coming up with nothing. Finally he finished.

"And you went in there even though it said 'No trespassing'?" Jaden asked.

"I had to follow the guy," Josh said.

"So you saw an old house and a guy who yelled at you after you almost made him crack up his truck? How does that equate to cheating?" she said, throwing her hands up and turning to go. "Hopefully for you, Josh, you won't get in trouble for trespassing."

"Jaden, hey, wait," Josh said, hurrying to catch up and seeing Lido step out of the ice-cream store and head their way with two cones, licking them alternately. "You can't tell me you didn't see what I saw in that game?"

She spun on him, her face pinched and red. "Tell me a baseball game where the losing team doesn't say the ump robbed them. You can't. That's right, it always happens. So you see Myron and the ump, so? That ump is Justin Seevers, the head umpire for the tournament. I met him before the game. Myron was probably coordinating the media for the next couple games and making sure the umpires who call the Comets games are okay with it. They're talking about using footage in some movie. He gave Seevers an envelope, right?"

"Yes," Josh said.

"Full of money?"

"I think," Josh said, "for the payoff."

Before either of them could say another word, Benji popped up between them with two cones, handing the triple chocolate to Josh and putting his cone into Jaden's face.

"I thought they said Moose *Craps*," Benji said excitedly, "and I was like 'Dude, I know this is supposed to be some special Italian ice cream, but who wants to eat something with a name like Moose Craps?' and they're like 'No, dude, it's Moose *Tracks*, and I taste it—even though it looks like craps—and, hey, Jaden, you've got to try this."

Jaden pushed his hand away, but Benji held the cone up again, dabbing the end of her nose with it. Jaden growled and grabbed the ice-cream cone and smeared it right in his face before she stomped away.

Benji stood for a minute, wiping his face, licking his fingers, and staring sadly at the lump of ice cream melting on the sidewalk.

"Dude," he said, looking sadly at Josh, "what was that all about?"

Josh shrugged. Benji turned and stared through the window of the ice-cream store and the crowd of people. "That line took me forever," he said.

"You going back for more?" Josh asked. "I thought we were going to see the sights, the Babe, Doubleday Field."

Benji sighed and said, "You know I got to."

Benji's shoulders slumped as he went back inside for a fresh cone. Josh sat on the ledge and finished his ice cream, staring at the brick corner where Jaden had disappeared, thinking about how wrong things had gone. He wasn't sure exactly why, or what to do about it. He was startled when Myron suddenly rounded the corner with his face glazed in sweat.

"Hey," he said like some long-lost friend, "you're Josh, right?"

"Yes."

Myron reached out with a long arm and snatched a handful of Josh's T-shirt. He yanked him forward, close enough for Josh to smell the sickening sweetness of menthol cigarettes on Myron's breath. Josh tried to pull away, dropping his ice-cream cone, but Myron's grip only tightened and Josh could feel the collar of his T-shirt cutting into his skin. Myron's eyes lurked beneath his heavy brows, darting back and forth like roaches scrambling in a spotlight.

"Come on," he said, dragging Josh toward the black limo that cruised up next to the curb. "I just heard your little friend telling Mickey Junior a funny story. You and I need to talk."

CHAPTER THIRTY-ONE

"RELAX, YOU'RE FINE," MYRON said, easing back into the limo's seat and lighting a cigarette. "Don't pee your pants."

"My friend," Josh said. He sat on the bench seat sideways, and as the car pulled away he saw Benji burst out from the ice-cream shop with his new cone held high above his head like some kind of gold medal.

"The fat kid?" Myron asked, raising an eyebrow and motioning with his thumb. "He'll be fine too. That ice cream will keep his mouth busy for a minute or two. You and I need to talk, though."

"You're kidnapping me," Josh said. Sweat broke out under his arms.

"Don't be a punk," Myron said with a growl, blowing a cloud of menthol smoke his way. "We're not even

144

having this conversation."

Josh coughed.

"You think you saw something today?" Myron asked, smoke curling up from his nostrils. "You think you're going to mess with the outcome of this tournament? Try to sling some mud at one of the greatest baseball players who ever lived? Ha!"

Myron leaned forward with the cigarette dangling from his lower lip. "That's not how it works. We'll bury you and your old man so fast you'll think you're a tulip bulb. Do you know what those reporters would do to get an exclusive sit-down with Mickey Mullen on the set of his next movie? Mickey Mullen has the media eating out of his hand. We own the media. And if we ask, they'll paint a picture of you and your dad that'll make a cow patty look pretty."

"My dad's a good coach," Josh said. "He was a first-round pick out of high school."

Myron removed the cigarette from his mouth and flicked the ashes on the floor. He smiled from ear to ear and said, "You mean that old washed-up minor leaguer who tried to pump his kid full of steroids, then sold out his business partner to the cops so he could slip into his own deal with Nike? That dad?

"It's all how you look at it, see?"

Josh felt his face bunch up. Myron enraged him, but he also made him afraid. He wanted to punch him, but something so clearly sinister about the apelike man let

Josh know that he wouldn't last two seconds.

"You really want to win this tournament by cheating?" Josh asked.

Myron raised both eyebrows. "What's the difference how we win it? We'll win it. That's a story. That's life. The strong survive, kid. You think you're stronger than me? You think you can outsmart, out-hustle, or out-fight me? Make a move."

Myron stared at him with his beetle-black eyes until Josh dropped his head.

"Pull over," Myron said, pushing a button and talking into a speaker that Josh knew must go to the driver up front behind his partition of glass.

The car pulled over to the curb. They'd only gone two and a half blocks.

"Get out," Myron said, flinging open the door. "You don't say a word about any of this to anyone. You don't even let me catch you even looking at Mickey or his son cross-eyed or the only thing you and your dad will have going with Nike is the pair of used sneakers they give you at the rescue mission when you're living on the street. You better leave the girl alone, too, while you're at it."

Josh climbed out and stood on the curb. A shiver went down his spine as the long, dark car rounded the corner. When he got back to the ice-cream shop, Benji was gone. Josh peered around the corner and saw no sign of Jaden and Mickey on the bench, either, so he made his way back to the shuttle stop. As he turned the corner, he saw the powder blue bus just pulling away in a heavy gray cloud of diesel. He ran to catch it, but its gears roared and clanked, and Josh could just imagine the grumpy lady in her Red Sox cap sneering at him in the rearview mirror.

"Shoot," Josh said, knowing it would be another hour before he could get a ride back. He stuck his hands in his pockets and made his way to Pioneer Alley, where he poked around in the souvenir shops until it was time to catch the next bus.

The round, grumpy lady cackled at him softly as he stepped onto the bus along with a small crowd of people from the camp, some with the Titans, some not. Josh took a seat in the back corner, not interested in having a conversation and only able to think about the bad things he'd like to do to Jaden, knowing it was she who had said something in front of Myron. When he got back to the Beaver Valley Campsite, he found his parents down at the edge of the pond. His dad lay back on a blanket, coated in suntan lotion and filling out the lineup card for their next game, while Laurel splashed her feet in the water under the protective wing of his mom.

"Benji's looking for you," his mom said. "I told him to check the cabin. Is something wrong? You look upset."

"I missed the dang shuttle bus and had to wait around an hour for it," Josh said. "That's all."

"We'll be eating in about forty-five minutes," his father said without looking up from his coaching book.

"Then we got batting practice to get ready for tomorrow. I know you guys are thinking about the Comets, but we've got to beat the Toronto Eagles and this Corcoran kid, then two other good teams, or we won't even get to the Comets. We'll do a team campfire after practice. Should be fun."

Inside the cabin, Benji sat on the couch, munching on a bag of BBQ Fritos and staring at the wall in a daze.

"Hey," Benji said, looking up at him. "I don't know how the pioneers ever lived without TV. This place is boring me to tears. Where you been? I came out of Esposito's and all I see is melted ice cream."

"Have you seen Jaden?" Josh asked, scowling.

"Just when you did," Benji said, offering him the bag of Fritos.

Josh ignored the bag and turned to go.

"Dude," Benji said, catching up with him on the grass and hustling alongside as Josh strode down the line of cabins, "what's up with you?"

"She's a traitor," Josh said.

"You can do better than her anyway," Benji said. "Remember Sheila Conway? The blonde with the older boyfriend who loved you? That's more your speed. You're the man, Josh. You don't need Jaden Neidermeyer. So, where are you going?"

"To her cabin," Josh said. "If she's even there."

"I bet she is," Benji said. "I saw that white limo pull

up when I was looking for you. She got out and that Mickey the mullet head, maggot-face Mullen was, like, kissing her good-bye."

Josh stopped to look at Benji and said, "She *kissed* him?"

CHAPTER THIRTY-TWO

"WELL," BENJI SAID, HOLDING up his hands, "not exactly, but it was like that. I said to myself, I said, 'Dude, she is so going to kiss him.'"

"But, she didn't."

"No, but that's next, I'm telling you," Benji said, making kissing noises. "You don't look at each other standing there like that all smiling and everything when some serious kissing isn't just around the next bend. Trust me. I know about these things."

"How do you know?" Josh asked.

"Genetics," Benji said with a simple shrug. "I was built for this kind of stuff."

"Now I've heard everything," Josh said, heading for Jaden's cabin again.

"Yep," Benji said. "Ladies and home runs."

Josh kept going.

"What happened to you, anyway?" Benji asked, catching up. "You still didn't tell me."

"I was . . ." Josh said as the image of Myron's dark, shifty eyes lurking beneath their thick brows filled his brain. He could practically feel the man's iron grip. "I saw someone from behind, limping down the street. I thought it was that ump and I followed him."

"Did you see anything?" Benji asked.

"No," Josh said. "Wrong guy. And I can't believe you just left."

"I looked all over," Benji said. "Jaden and Mullet Head were gone, so I thought maybe you went with them or something. I didn't know. You didn't say anything. What was I supposed to do?"

"Nothing," Josh said. The two of them reached the tiny cabin belonging to Jaden and her father.

Josh put his hand on the railing and climbed the steps while Benji hung back. The cabin had a screen door and Josh could see right in. Dr. Neidermeyer was sitting at the small table working at his computer. When Josh knocked, Dr. Neidermeyer removed the small, round glasses from his face and rubbed his nose, telling him to come in.

"That's okay, Dr. Neidermeyer," Josh said. "I don't want to disturb you. I'm just looking for Jaden."

"Come in for a minute, will you, Josh?" Dr. Neidermeyer said. "I'd like to talk to you."

Josh looked back down the stairs just in time to see Benji ducking behind the side of the cabin. He shook his head and pushed open the creaky screen door.

"Soda?" Dr. Neidermeyer asked, pointing to a cooler on the floor.

"I'm okay, Dr. Neidermeyer," Josh said.

"Sit. Please."

Josh sat down and looked at his sneakers.

"Josh, I don't want to be that dad that gets involved in everything his daughter is doing," Dr. Neidermeyer said, "but Jaden's all I really have, and without her mom, well, I guess I worry for two parents. I know how much she likes you and, well, I hate to put you in a bad spot, but something's wrong with her and for the first time in her life, she won't talk to me about it. I know you two have been through a lot together, with that Rocky Valentine thing and the steroids and all, and I know there's no one in the world she cares about more than you. There isn't anything she wouldn't do for you. So, I'm sorry, but can you tell me what's going on?"

"Why do you say something is wrong?" Josh asked.

"Because when I asked her," Dr. Neidermeyer said, "she ran out of here crying. I went looking for her, to make sure she was okay, and I saw her on the walking trail down by the stream, just sitting there on a rock, looking into the water. I thought it was best to let her be for now. I came back to try and do some work, but all

I'm really thinking about is her. Can you tell me what's wrong?"

Josh looked up at the doctor's pleasant face. He was a thin man with straight dark hair that hung in a small mess. The only physical quality he and Jaden seemed to share was their gold-flecked green eyes. Josh had never seen him look so sad.

"I think I should talk to her to make sure myself," Josh said. "That's kind of why I came."

Dr. Neidermeyer studied him for a moment before nodding and saying, "If you follow those red markers through the woods, it'll take you right to her."

Josh thanked him and trod down the steps. He was halfway to the woods when Benji caught up to him.

"Dude, what happened?" Benji asked. "Does he know she's hooked up with Maggot Head? Where is she?"

"Let me go find Jaden by myself," Josh said. "I'll meet you back at the cabin for dinner."

Benji took hold of Josh's arm and said, "You gotta promise me one thing, Josh. I'll go, but you gotta be strong. You gotta put Jaden in her place, at the back of the line. You can't let her smile at you like she can do and you melt like popcorn butter. You gotta be firm and tell her the deal, how she betrayed her friends for some California mope. With his tan and his girly looks and all his money and private jets and mansions and all that crap. That doesn't go with us Syracuse boys.

We're straight up. That's what you gotta tell her."

"And I will," Josh said, pointing back toward the cabins. "But alone. I've got to do it alone, Benji."

"'Cause you just said she was a traitor but now you look kind of mushy," Benji said.

"Trust me."

"I just care about you, man," Benji said, nodding wisely. "I know it's tough. I know all about girls and what they can do to you, get you in their spell and all that, but if you can break free, it'll be better in the long run. You're the man, Josh. You deserve someone who'd walk on water for you."

"You mean walk through fire?" Josh said.

Benji looked at him with serious eyes and said, "That too, brother. I mean both."

Benji held up his hand, Josh slapped him five, they clasped hands, and Benji pulled him into a hug before breaking away and disappearing back down the path.

Josh turned and followed the trail. The trees soon thinned, and he saw the rocky stream. Sunlight filtered through the leaves, and the gurgling water calmed his nerves. Jaden sat with her back to him atop a giant boulder, staring at her reflection in a flat pool of water.

Josh walked up to her and cleared his throat.

Jaden jumped and spun, slipping from the rock and stumbling into the shallow pool of water, shattering its still surface. Her expression changed from shock to anger before crumbling into a tortured sob.

"Josh," she said, leaning toward him, "I did something horrible."

CHAPTER THIRTY-THREE

JADEN HUGGED HIM, AND Josh kept his hands stiff to his sides. She was crying.

"You told Mickey Junior what I saw right in front of Myron," Josh said quietly.

She nodded her head against his shoulder.

"I know," Josh said. "He paid me a visit."

Jaden separated from him, holding his elbows. "Are you okay?"

"For now," Josh said, shrugging. "He basically told me to keep out of it or I'd be sorry."

"He threatened you?"

"He said the whole thing never happened," Josh said. "He said if I made any noise, the media would do a big story on my dad and make him look really bad. He said Nike would never get near him again and that we'd be living on the street."

Jaden groaned. "I was so stupid. I thought Myron would just laugh and say how crazy it was, but instead he got this insane look on his face and I *knew*. When I said something to Mickey Junior, he just laughed it off and said something about his dad being a little too competitive sometimes. I'm sorry, Josh. I'm so sorry."

Josh shrugged.

"You're mad," she said, turning away. "I know."

"I was mad," Josh said. "But if you're sorry, then I can't stay mad."

She turned back to him, glowing. "I appreciate that."

"Yeah," Josh said softly. "That's okay."

He took a deep breath, smelling the warm scent of bark and pine needles and feeling things between them shift back to the old way.

Finally he said, "I still feel all twisted up inside, though. I can't believe they're going to win this tournament by paying off the umpires. That is so bad. I was hoping we could win this thing. Nike told my dad he'd get a five-year contract if we did."

"What are you going to do?" Jaden asked.

Josh shrugged and said, "Just play and hopefully make it to the championship and then they'll roll over us. Like Myron said to me, that's not how it works."

"Because you don't want Myron coming after you," Jaden said.

"Honestly? That guy is scary," Josh said. "Even if I could prove it, which I don't see how I can, there's no way I'm going to have him coming after me for telling people about them cheating."

"But you don't have to tell people," Jaden said.

"What are you talking about?" he asked.

"It's bad enough they're doing this," Jaden said, "but it's a hundred times worse if I'm the one who helped them, even if it wasn't on purpose. You don't have to be the one to tell everyone and ruin their plan.

"I will."

CHAPTER THIRTY-FOUR

AS THE WEEK WENT on, the weather stayed nice—bright blue skies, puffy clouds, and warm afternoon sun washed over the mountains, woods, and baseball fields. Whether they hit home runs or dropped pop flies, the players all found their eyes drawn over and over to the college scouts who wore caps from their various universities and jotted down endless notes.

Josh and the Titans won their second game, overcoming the Toronto Eagles and Chase Corcoran's slider. Josh was surprised when he looked up into the stands during the game to see Mickey Mullen Jr. scouting the Titans, but instead of being a distraction, Josh used the rival's presence to spur him on to another stellar performance. By the time it was over, Josh had hit five home runs between the first two games, resulting in several interviews for television stations as well as newspapers. The matchup between his bat and Mickey Mullen Jr.'s pitching seemed to be growing into a major story.

Wednesday afternoon the entire Dream Park was abuzz with news of Mickey Jr.'s no-hitter that morning and the Comets' advancement to the semifinals. Josh felt the challenge and rose to the occasion himself in their afternoon quarterfinal game against a team from Dallas. Josh went three for four, belting two out of the park and helping to get the Titans one game closer to the big matchup. After the game, a man in sunglasses and a faded denim shirt and jeans approached Josh.

"Some game, buddy," the man said. "At least the Mullen kid might have some competition somewhere in this thing. I'm Stu Lisson. I'm a producer for Bob Costas."

The man named Stu angled his head over his shoulder at field seven—the place where Mickey Jr. had pitched his no-hitter for the Comets earlier in the day—but Josh forgot about his rival, feeling instead a pulse of excitement at the name Bob Costas, one of the most famous sports announcers ever.

"We're doing a piece on Mickey Mullen and his son for HBO," Stu said. "The kid is something. You heard about that no-hitter he pitched this morning, right?"

"Yeah," Josh said flatly. "I heard about it."

"Incredible. But we keep hearing about you Titans guys, too, and you in particular," Stu said. "Five home runs in two games? And then we were over there shooting some B-roll and I heard you got two more today? And that scar."

Josh touched the smooth ridge beneath his eye.

"Did you really have a plate put in your face just so you could play?" Stu asked.

Josh nodded, thinking how it would look on TV.

Stu got a faraway look in his eyes and seemed to have read Josh's mind when he said, "See, that's great. Shows how much you love this game. Bob loves a kid with passion for the sport. So, we know it's not certain, but if you win the next one and the Comets stay on track, it'll be you guys facing off in the championship. Bob wants to get a counterpoint to Mickey Junior for the show. A rival. Make it like some kind of monster movie, you know?"

Josh felt his scar again, wondering if he meant Josh looked like a monster.

"King Kong versus Godzilla?" Stu said, without seeming to notice Josh's discomfort. "Predator versus Alien? People love that stuff. Someone told me that your dad used to play a little baseball too, so that could be another nice angle. Rich vs. Poor. Famous vs. the Unknown."

"He played for thirteen years in the pros," Josh said, forgetting his scar and raising his chin. "Now he's our coach."

Stu began to smile, then nodded seriously. "In the minors, right? It doesn't matter. The thing is you two kids. Both of you pretty advanced for your ages. Both with dads who . . . played. So, we're thinking—if you keep winning—a kind of round table interview with you two and Bob for *Inside Sports*. What do you think?"

CHAPTER THIRTY-FIVE

JOSH'S PARENTS SAID THAT of course he could do the interview, but his dad wasn't as excited as Josh thought he'd be about Josh meeting and being interviewed for HBO by Bob Costas.

"Oh, Costas is great," his dad said on the bus ride back to the camp. "One of my favorite announcers. A legend. But that media stuff is harder than it looks."

"What?" Josh said. "You just answer the questions, be yourself. What could be hard?"

His dad gave him a funny look, then shrugged. "Well, if you're gonna be in the big leagues one day, you might as well learn the ropes right now. It's a great opportunity. Bob Costas and HBO is about as big as it gets. We have to beat the South Carolina team in the semifinals first, though. If nothing else, it'll give you a good incentive."

"Come on, Dad," Josh said. "Winning is all the incentive I need, right?"

His dad smiled hard at that and nodded his approval.

The next day it rained, but the tournament had built two days into the schedule for just such possibilities, so it was no big deal. Josh's dad had the team bus take them all on a trip to the Farmers' Museum. While everyone groaned about it at first, they actually ended up enjoying the trip because of a real live blacksmith who put on a show with sparks and steam and red-hot iron. Afterward they all went to the Southside Mall in Oneonta for a movie before returning to the camp for dinner.

Josh and his family sat down with Jaden and her dad along with Benji, but Jaden said few words. It wasn't until afterward, when Benji had returned to the cabin to use the bathroom and Josh waited with Jaden for her limo ride to yet another media party, that he was able to quiz her on what she'd found out during the day.

"Nothing from Mickey Junior or his dad," Jaden said, shaking her head and looking off into the meadow, where fireflies blinked in the high grass. "They spent most of the day in their suite playing Xbox Three-sixty with all kinds of people hanging around. Neither said a word about Seevers, and I didn't even see Myron. Honestly, Josh? In their game yesterday, if I didn't know about what you saw? I would never have guessed there was some kind of bribery going on. I mean, he made a couple questionable calls, but nothing anyone went crazy about."

Josh frowned and said, "Yeah, but they blew that team away, right? It would make sense that he only makes the calls if they need him to. Kind of an insurance policy to make sure they win for the whole media show. It's like making a movie for Mickey Mullen. You gotta admit that it's strange that he'd be the umpire for all the Comets games to begin with."

"Right," she said, "so I looked into Seevers a bit. First of all, I didn't even know this, but there are no standards or anything for umpires in Little League Baseball. It's just whoever's done it before and at local levels. A lot of times that's just high school kids or dads who're willing to put up with the grief. I talked to a couple people around town and the word on the guy is that he inherited that house from his dead wife's family and doesn't put a dime into it. He runs a ski resort down in Pennsylvania, then he heads off to Las Vegas and usually loses everything he made before coming here for the summer."

Jaden looked around to scope out the shadows surrounding them before continuing. "Seevers umpires while he's here to make extra money, been doing it for years, and all of a sudden the head umpire for the tournament bailed out. Seevers made a big pitch for the job and he'd been umping summer games for years, so they gave it to him. Because he's the head umpire, he controls the schedule, so it's easy to make sure he works all the Comets games. I'm sure people figure he does it just to be around the excitement, the cameras and all that, not to cheat. Also, I checked the snow reports from last winter and I'm betting Seevers *really* needs the money this year because temperatures were the warmest they've been in twenty-seven years and the snow total was half what it normally is."

"So," Josh said. "He lives in a run-down house with its own graveyard, he gambles and usually loses, and we think that somehow Mickey Mullen offered him something he couldn't refuse. Money."

Jaden shrugged and looked up at the star-filled sky.

"And all the guy has to do is make a couple really crappy calls," Josh said, "which happens all the time anyway."

"Only not on purpose," Jaden said, directing her stare at him. "I don't know, Josh. Even with all the circumstantial evidence, we still need to prove it. That's the key."

"How'd you find out all this stuff, anyway?" Josh asked.

"I keep telling you," Jaden said. "I'm a reporter."

"Right," Josh said, nodding. "I know that. Like Bob Costas."

"I met him," Jaden said.

"Was he nice?" Josh asked.

"Yes," she said, "but it's like he's so smart he can look right into your head and see the wheels turning."

"Great," Josh said. "That's all I need, a guy looking right through me in a TV interview."

"You're nervous?" Jaden asked as the headlight beams from the approaching limo flashed across them.

"I wasn't," Josh said, touching his scar. "Then my dad gave me this 'It's a lot harder than it looks' speech. Mickey Junior grew up with the cameras in his face. I don't want to look like some goofball sitting there choking on my own spit."

"Just breathe deep," Jaden said as the car pulled to a stop and the driver got out to open the door. "That's what they say, anyway."

"And this scar," Josh said.

"You'll be fine," Jaden said, sliding into the backseat.

"Sure. Have fun," Josh said.

"It's work, really," Jaden said. "You don't get that, but thanks."

The driver closed the door, rounded the car, and the limo pulled away. Benji appeared, still drying his hands on a wad of paper towels.

Benji stared at the car until it disappeared around the bend, then said, "You ever think that she might be working for the enemy?"

"The Comets?"

"That's their limo she's riding around in," Benji said.

"I think she's just doing her job, Benji," Josh said, thinking of the plan he and Jaden had worked out together. "She's our friend."

"Yeah," Benji said. "That's true. But with women? Buddy, anything's possible. Anything at all."

CHAPTER THIRTY-SIX

EVEN THOUGH THE COMETS weren't playing their semifinal game until Saturday morning, the Titans played theirs on Friday afternoon. Josh nailed a single and blasted two more home runs to help them beat a team from South Carolina by a run. The Titans went crazy, screaming to one another how great they were and chanting "Championship, championship, championship" over and over. Stu Lisson was the first person to greet Josh after the excitement had waned and he left the dugout with his bat bag. "Nice," Stu said, clapping Josh on the shoulder and grinning at his dad. "So, what do you think, Mr. LeBlanc? Can we shoot that interview tonight?"

"But the Comets aren't in it for sure, yet," Josh said, the words escaping his mouth before he could even think.

Stu gave him a funny smile, then said, "Yeah, their semi's tomorrow, but the way they've been looking, we feel pretty comfortable with going ahead anyway."

Stu turned back to Josh's dad and said, "The Mullens are on board and they'll fly Josh down to New York this afternoon in their private jet. We'll shoot the round table and have him back here by eight or nine at the latest. You good?"

Josh looked up at his dad. The thought of flying in a private jet and going to New York City for an HBO interview with Bob Costas made him forget all about the scandal he hoped to uncover, as well as the ill feelings he had for Mickey Mullen and his son.

"I'll just have to check in with his mom," Josh's dad said. "Today sounds good to me, though. A great opportunity."

"Of course," Stu said. "You check with the missus and let me know. I'll give you my cell number. If your wife is worried about him being alone, we can have Mickey Junior's girlfriend fly down too. She's with your hometown paper, right?"

Josh's stomach twisted at the description of Jaden as Mickey Jr.'s girlfriend.

"That would probably be nice," his dad said.

"Sure," Stu said, "she's practically part of the Mullen entourage. Bob likes her spirit, too, says she's a real firecracker."

CHAPTER THIRTY-SEVEN

TWO HOURS LATER JOSH was sitting with Jaden in the back of the big white limousine that she seemed quite comfortable in. Josh's mom had dressed him in a white button-down dress shirt, a pair of dark blue pants, and black shoes for the occasion. Josh felt like he was going to church, but he trusted his mom when she said he needed to look good for the camera. Several times during the ride he cleared his throat to say something to Jaden about the girlfriend thing, but for some reason he couldn't bring himself to do it.

"You feeling okay?" Jaden asked. She wore jeans and a pink polo shirt, but she wasn't going to be on camera.

"Great," he said.

"You keep coughing and touching your scar."

171

Josh left his face alone, faked another cough, and patted his chest. "My allergies."

"I didn't know you have allergies," she said.

"Just a little sometimes," Josh said, and turned his attention to the green trees whizzing by outside the window and to forcing his hands to stay at his sides.

When the limo pulled out onto the tarmac of the small airfield, Josh rolled down the window to get a better look at the plane. It looked like a white shark with wings. Engines the size of refrigerators framed its tail. The skin of the plane caught the afternoon light and flung it back at Josh's eyes, making it hard to look at the big machine for more than a glance.

On board Mickey Mullen talked on a cell phone as he sat in a beige leather reclining seat beside Myron Underwood. But even Myron's mean look couldn't dampen the excitement Josh felt as Mickey Mullen slapped him a high five while he followed Jaden up the short aisle past a handful of other people to the back, where Mickey Jr. sat in one of four seats facing each other. Josh looked at Mickey Jr.'s sneakers, tattered jeans, and gray hoodie before he fumbled to undo the top button of his dress shirt. Mickey Jr. was playing on a Nintendo DX, hammering away at it for another couple minutes while Jaden and Josh buckled in and just stared around at the shiny reddish brown wood, brass fixtures, and soft leather upholstery.

When he finished his game, Mickey Jr. tucked the PSP into the big front pocket of his sweatshirt and signaled to the flight attendant up in the front. The plane began to roll down the runway as she appeared and he ordered sandwiches and sodas for them all. She nodded and returned to her seat, buckling in.

The plane's engines roared suddenly and they catapulted down the runway. Josh gripped the armrests of his seat as they rocketed nearly straight up. Once they leveled out, the sandwiches came. Josh waited until Mickey Jr. took one off the tray before reaching into the pile himself. The roast beef and American cheese seemed to melt in Josh's mouth almost without chewing, and soon they were flying high above the clouds and picking at a second tray of strawberries dipped in dark chocolate. Without being obvious, Josh tried to follow Mickey Jr.'s lead on virtually everything. But while Mickey Jr. seemed relaxed and right at home, Josh knew his own speech, like his actions, was stiff and uneasy.

After a nose-dive landing and a short taxi on the runway, they all got off and boarded two limousines that rushed the entire group into New York City through the Lincoln Tunnel. Josh couldn't help feeling important as he stepped out of the limousine and marched along with the rest of the group into the HBO studios.

After passing the security desk without stopping, they all rode up an elevator together, then went down a long hall. Josh could see Mickey Mullen up ahead of the group with people orbiting around him like he was the sun, even as he moved.

They were shown into a room full of comfortable couches where the coffee tables and cabinets along the walls had been lined with more trays of elegant food and drinks. Josh sat on a couch next to Jaden. Mickey Jr. sat on her other side and removed the Nintendo DX from his sweatshirt front pocket. He joked to Jaden that he was addicted to it before he began to play.

Josh leaned close to Jaden, his eyes on the pale yellow walls, and said, "I heard someone say this is the green room, but it's yellow."

Jaden smiled and glanced at Mickey Jr. before she leaned toward Josh and in a low voice said, "They call it a green room. It's just a TV term for the waiting room before you go on air or into a shoot."

Josh nodded like he knew that.

It wasn't long before a woman in jeans and thick plastic glasses appeared with a clipboard and asked for Josh and Mickey Jr. to come with her to makeup. Jaden followed, and Josh cast a look at her over his shoulder with a questioning shrug. She didn't get to answer before they were whisked into a room that could have been a small hair salon with its three barber chairs facing a mirror and counter covered with scissors, blow dryers, hair products, and boxes of makeup.

Josh looked over at Mickey Jr., who had slumped himself down in a chair and continued to play even as a young woman—a makeup artist—with orange hair draped a plastic cape around his neck. Josh sat in the

next chair and watched as a second woman—a hairstylist—picked up a pair of scissors and began to snip
at his hair. Too nervous to complain or even ask how
much she planned to cut, Josh watched in the mirror
as the makeup artist applied makeup to Mickey Jr.'s
face. The hairstylist stood back, primping his hair, and
then told him to close his eyes as she unloaded a cloud
of spray onto his head.

When the makeup artist finished with Mickey Jr.,
she swapped places with the hairstylist and bent over
so that her face hung just over Josh's shoulder as she
looked at him in the mirror.

"Umm," she said, directing one of her long pink and
white nails toward his cheek, "I'll do my best to cover
this, but I don't think I can hide it all."

"No, no," the woman with the clipboard said, stepping in from the doorway to speak to the makeup artist.
"Stu wants the scar. Don't cover the scar. They love it."

Josh looked nervously at the makeup artist's expression of surprise, wondering if she too worried that they
were making him out to be some kind of freak.

"Oh," she said. "Sure."

As the makeup artist began to paint Josh's face
with several types of makeup, brush his eyebrows, and
dust him up with powder, Josh tried not to breathe
the strange-smelling stuff through his nose. His stomach clenched, and he cast a worried look at Jaden. He
expected her to grin at the silliness of him getting made

up, but she didn't seem to notice. Her eyes were on Mickey Jr., and when Josh compared his own scarred face in the mirror to Mickey's, he remembered Stu Lisson's words about a monster movie.

Before Josh knew it, they were being shuttled into the studio, where Bob Costas sat at a table studying the papers in front of him. Josh took the remaining seat around the dark, granite-topped table. An audio person clipped a microphone to his shirt collar, running the wire down through his shirt and around his pants before plugging it into a small battery pack that he'd clipped to Josh's belt. The set, a raised platform covered with carpet, was an oasis of light in a forest of huge cameras, bare metal beams, and a tangle of cables.

Josh stared around at the hot white lights and tried to swallow, even though his tongue, dry and sticky, seemed to have swollen to twice its usual size. Suddenly Bob Costas upended his papers and tapped their bottom edges against the table as he looked at Josh and Mickey Jr.

"You guys ready?" he asked.

Josh stared back at the famous announcer's serious face and penetrating eyes. His throat started to tickle and before he could nod or say yes, he began to cough. The woman with the clipboard rushed out from behind the bright lights and handed him a bottle of water. Josh drank half of it down and realized he had to use the bathroom.

"Okay now?" Bob Costas asked with real concern. "You look a little nervous. Just relax. You'll be fine."

Josh nodded, even though the last thing he felt was fine.

"Uh," Bob Costas said to someone beyond the lights, "can someone bring a bucket?"

Josh's stomach churned, and he tasted the roast beef and cheese as it gurgled up from his belly on a wave of soda.

CHAPTER THIRTY-EIGHT

JOSH HEAVED HIS LUNCH into a wastepaper basket with a mighty spatter. He choked and coughed, heaved again, then took a swig from his water bottle to wash the vile taste from his mouth. He wiped the corners of his lips on the back of his wrist. The makeup artist hurried onto the set with a wet towel, dabbing his face before reapplying the powder.

Josh felt his face flush with embarrassment. He glanced over at where Jaden stood, knowing it was her only by the jeans and pink polo shirt. The bright lights blotted out her face and he worried at what her expression must be, but not for long. Bob Costas introduced both Josh and Mickey Jr. in glowing terms, then started asking questions as if nothing unusual had happened. Mickey Jr., too, carried on as if the three of them were hanging around the kitchen table. Josh watched in wonder as the two of them chatted. When a question came his way, he struggled to choke out a couple words and his face only grew hotter.

After several minutes Stu Lisson walked out onto the set, interrupting Bob and kneeling beside Josh so he could speak into his ear.

"Hey," Stu said in a pleasant whisper, "we love the scar and the whole story behind it, but you gotta leave it alone, okay? Maybe sit on your hands?"

"Oh sure," Josh said, nodding fervently, dropping his hands, and parking them under his legs, mortified that he'd been picking at his face without even knowing it.

"Okay, great," Stu said, standing up with a wink and a thumbs-up. "Doing good, Josh. Breathe deep."

Josh nodded some more and tried to follow the advice he remembered Jaden had given him and now the producer, too.

"Okay?" Bob Costas said, looking up into the lights. "Rolling again?"

Bob Costas touched his ear, nodded, and started in again, asking questions and looking—just as Jaden had said he would—right into Josh's and Mickey Jr.'s brains at the wheels. Josh knew his own wheels were rusty and broken down, especially when asked to speak about the heroic operation he had in order to play in the national championship. Then, flustered as he was, Josh suddenly understood that his role in the interview was one of the hopeless underdog and not the baseball rival.

As Mickey Jr. finished explaining why the Comets were such huge favorites to win, Josh straightened his back and raised his chin.

"Well, Josh," Bob Costas said, turning to him when Mickey Jr. had finished, "it'll be a tall order for your Titans to stand up to the Comets."

"With all due respect, Mr. Costas," Josh said without wavering, "talk is cheap, and champions are like blue moons. They don't come around much. Me and the rest of the Titans are planning on winning the big one."

Bob Costas paused for a moment, then blinked before a smile crept onto his face. "Well said, Josh. That's why we play the game, right? To see who that champion is going to be."

"He doth protest too much," Mickey Jr. said, smirking.

"Quoting Shakespeare now, Mickey?" Bob Costas said, obviously enjoying the literary reference. "What do you mean?"

"Josh is busy telling us how they plan on winning the big one," Mickey Jr. said, "because he knows he's the underdog."

"I'm okay with being an underdog," Josh said, his chin still high. "This country was built by underdogs. It's as American as baseball and apple pie."

Bob Costas beamed. "Oh yes."

Mickey Jr. seemed at a loss before he said, "That was then, this is now."

"Right," Josh said, feeling himself run out of clever things to say.

"But now America stands alone," Mickey Jr. said, grinning at himself as he gained the upper hand once again. "We're the only superpower left in the world. They say every dog has its day; well, the underdog had its day already. Now we live in an age of champions, dynasties, and superpowers, and that's what the Comets are."

Bob Costas gave Josh a second to say something, but when it became clear he had nothing left to add, the famous announcer wished them both luck. As the audio man unclipped his microphone, Josh breathed a sigh of relief, thinking that at least he'd gotten a couple things right.

The flight back to Cooperstown was a blur, but with every passing minute, Josh's clever words seemed to fade as the faltering end of the interview took center stage in his mind. Josh spent the trip with his head hanging low between both hands. He had a headache and used that as his excuse not to talk. Everyone left him alone, either out of thoughtfulness or a lack of concern, and to Josh it didn't matter. The most uncomfortable part was when he rode alone with Jaden in the back of the limo. She tried to talk to him a couple times and even spoke with encouragement about how they could edit the show to keep only the best of his answers.

Josh couldn't even respond. The smell of vomit, his stumbling words, and, in the end, his inability to even speak haunted him. Finally Jaden gave up trying, and they stared out their separate windows as the long car rolled through the countryside's fading light. Somehow the pressure seemed less after he mumbled good night to Jaden and she disappeared down the gravel path toward her cabin.

Josh watched her go, his mind now turning to the game and how they might win it despite the odds. He'd need to be at his best, and as he replayed his finest moment in the interview and Bob Costas's reply about why they played the game, Josh took heart.

When he went into his own cabin, Josh did his best to answer his parents' and Benji's questions but used the same headache to make quick work of them. His dad was kind enough not to say "I told you so" as Josh recounted how bad things had really gone, except for his last answer. When he finally closed the door to his tiny cabin bedroom, Josh climbed up into his bunk and lay staring at the ceiling.

The door opened quietly, and Benji lay down on the bottom bunk without a word. Josh waited for several minutes before he spoke.

"You don't have to stay with me," Josh said, even though Benji's presence somehow comforted him.

"Ah, that's okay," Benji said. "You can only watch so

many campfires and eat so many s'mores. My hair's starting to smell like smoke. I liked how you said you ended that thing with Costas, the stuff about talk being cheap."

Josh smiled in the dark.

"Anyway," Benji said brightly, "forget about all that TV stuff. We got a game to play on Sunday, right? We're in the championship. Who knows if Mullet Head Mullen will even get there. They gotta win tomorrow. We're already in."

Josh sighed and said, "They seem pretty confident."

"I'd be confident too if I had the umpire in my back pocket," Benji said.

"Hopefully with Jaden's help we can put a stop to all that," Josh said, but even in the small, dark bedroom, just him and his best friend, the words sounded weak and without meaning.

CHAPTER THIRTY-NINE

THE NEXT MORNING, SATURDAY, Josh, Benji, Josh's dad, and the entire team went to watch the other semifinal game together. The Comets faced a dynamite team from Houston called the Roughriders, and it wasn't easy to find a seat. They had to climb all the way to the top corner of the bleachers in the section dominated by Houston fans.

TV cameras were everywhere.

Because the Comets were saving Mickey Jr. to pitch in what they hoped would be the championship game, two of their other pitchers shared duty on the mound. Meanwhile, Mickey Jr. played first base. At first it seemed to Josh that Seevers was allowing the Comets pitchers a much bigger strike zone than the team from Houston, and from the shouts and jeers of the Houston fans around him, Josh knew he wasn't the only one who thought so. But the advantage was a subtle one, and Jaden's words about baseball fans always complaining about the calls when they were losing came into Josh's mind. It was funny, but the most conclusive proof they had of cheating was Myron's reaction to what Josh had seen.

As the score began to widen, the strike zone for the Comets pitchers seemed to shrink. The Comets had a powerful offense led by Mickey Jr., who hit two singles, one of them earning an RBI, and even a home run with two runners on. Before the end of the fourth inning, the Comets enjoyed an 8–3 lead. Josh ached to see something amiss but had to admit to himself that in the fifth and sixth innings, Seevers called an even game. Still, the Houston team could only score two additional runs, and even though it looked like the Roughriders might rally, the Comets won 8–5, making it official: Sunday's final game for the Hall of Fame trophy and the national championship would take place between the LA Comets and the Syracuse Titans.

"Well, it's the rivalry they all wanted to see, you against Mickey Mullen Junior. HBO's gotta be happy," Josh's dad said before turning his attention to the notebook he had in his lap and jotting down some final thoughts that Josh knew he'd process later when he was developing his strategy for the championship game.

As they sat waiting for the crowd to disperse and

the teams shook hands over home plate, Benji leaned toward Josh, pointing at the far dugout, and in a whisper said, "Look at her. Can you believe this? Another one."

Josh followed Benji's finger to see Jaden sitting by herself in the Comets dugout, writing what Josh guessed would be some final thoughts in her notepad. Benji removed a copy of the *Post-Standard*'s sports page from the day before that he'd kept rolled up in his back pocket and slapped it against the bleachers' wooden seat. It was the page from that morning with a big color picture of Mickey Mullen Jr. on it. Another photo, the size of a postage stamp, showed the smiling face of Jaden, the author of the big story about Mickey Jr. and his no-hitter.

"*We* get into the championship game," Benji said with a growl, "and all she can write about is surfer boy."

"You don't see many no-hitters," Josh said, doing his best to stay positive, forcing himself not to think of Jaden as a double agent, despite her focus on Mickey Jr.'s achievement from two days ago.

"With *that* guy's strike zone you do," Benji said with a grunt at the umpire who was leaving the field. "*I* could throw a no-hitter if he was on my payroll. What's she going to do when this tournament is over? Move to Hollywood? When we're all home and she comes crawling back, I promise you she gets no sympathy, right?"

Benji nudged Josh in the ribs. "Right?"

"I don't know, Benji," Josh said, tugging at his cap. "Sometimes you have to have blind trust, move on. My mom's always saying it's better not to carry bitterness around with you. It's like poison that gets in your blood."

"Well, my blood's good and red," Benji said, digging his paw into a box of popcorn and filling his face.

"What's that got to do with it?" Josh asked.

"Like a red-blooded American," Benji said through a mouthful of corn.

"Yeah? And?" Josh said, looking at him quizzically, wondering what the connection was until he realized there was none.

"Well," Josh said to Benji, standing up to get out of there and ready to change the subject, "it's official. Titans versus Comets for the national championship."

"Bring it on," Benji said.

Josh nodded, then winced as Mickey Jr. returned from a swarm of cameras to the dugout. He slapped his famous father a high five, then gave Jaden a hug. As Josh watched, the evil thoughts crept back into his mind.

CHAPTER FORTY

JOSH AND BENJI LET Josh's dad block for them as they navigated through the crowd toward the parking lot. As they funneled past the fence next to first base, Benji stopped and pointed to the sky.

"Look," he said.

Josh shaded his eyes and looked up for the source of a thundering noise that grew louder by the second. The windows of a tar black helicopter glinted like diamonds as the aircraft floated down toward the outfield. When it landed, Josh did a double take at what he saw. Crouched behind Mickey Mullen, Mickey Jr., and Myron was Jaden, scurrying beneath the spinning blades and hopping into the helicopter with the rest. A couple of cameramen and photographers spilled out onto the field to get a shot as the big bird whined and lifted itself off the grass. The wind from the helicopter swept dust from the baseline into their eyes and mouths. Benji coughed dramatically and swatted the air in front of his face.

"What the heck was that?" Benji asked. "I thought you and her were on good terms again."

"We are."

Benji squinted up at the copter as it leveled off and whooshed away in the direction of town. "Not as good as Mickey Junior, I guess. At least until you can give her a helicopter ride, huh?"

Josh's father had stopped to watch along with everyone else, and he gave Josh a wave with his head and continued on through the enormous crowd. They got onto the team bus with the rest of the Titans and waited in the hot, dusty traffic as the lot emptied out onto Route 28.

Josh's dad stood up in front of the bus and asked, "What does everyone think? Into town to catch the sights, or back to the camp for some swimming? I'd like to have some batting practice, but I think we'll wait until tomorrow morning and get our groove for the finals tomorrow afternoon."

Almost everyone agreed that they'd rather go back and swim, so, despite Josh's pleading, the bus headed away from town when they reached Route 28.

"Aren't you tired of the Hall of Fame?" Josh's dad asked.

"It's not just that," Josh said. "It's the town. Ice

cream, Doubleday Field, the shops. It's Cooperstown, Dad. It's the mecca of baseball."

"No more souvenirs," Josh's dad said. "Enough already. You can take the shuttle bus if you want to go that bad."

"Dude," Benji said, "can we give it a rest? I am so sick of that old bag's face. Let's swim."

Josh didn't say anything. He reached up into the luggage carrier and pulled a copy of *Watership Down* from his bat bag before sitting down in the window seat.

"You're just going to sit there and read about rabbits?" Benji said with a look of disbelief as he took the seat beside Josh.

Josh considered him for a moment before he said, "If I tell you something, can you keep a secret for a change?"

"A change?" Benji said, screwing up his face. "I'm like the Finks, dude."

Josh blinked. "The *Sphinx*? You mean the Egyptian Sphinx, the monument that's guarded the secrets of the pyramids for thousands of years, right?"

"I mean whatever keeps secrets like no one else," Benji said, raising his chin. "That's me."

Josh took a deep breath and said, "Jaden and I have a plan."

"What plan?" Benji asked.

"The plan I want to tell you about that I want you to keep secret."

"When did you come up with a plan?" Benji asked.

"The day you dumped your ice-cream cone."

"With Jaden?"

"Yes."

"And you're not telling me until now?" Benji asked.

"It's a secret."

"Not from me," Benji said. "You don't keep secrets from me."

"I'm not. I'm telling you."

"Because the plan has obviously failed," Benji said, poking his thumb in the direction of the sky where the helicopter had disappeared. "Mainly because you didn't have the Heavy Hitter in on it. What were you thinking?"

Josh told him how Jaden was supposed to be getting inside information so they could catch Myron in the act of paying off Seevers.

Benji cleared his throat and gave Josh a somber look. "Did you ever think maybe she's just tricking us? Like a double agent? One of those spies who pretends to be on your side but really they're spying on *you*."

"Pretending to go along with us but really protecting Mickey Junior?" Josh asked, shaking his head, even though he worried about the same thing. "Come on, Lido. She told me all about who the umpire is and why he's doing this."

"That's what double agents do," Benji said. "They give you a little bit here and there to keep you thinking they're on your side. What about that article she wrote in the Syracuse paper all about the Comets? I thought she was supposed to be here to do stories on our team. Heck, she and her dad rode the team bus down here with us."

"She writes what they ask her for," Josh said.

"Did they ask her to fly around in a helicopter with surfer boy?" Benji said.

"You don't think she'd lie to me just to keep me quiet, do you?" Josh asked. "I don't think she'd do that, but then I see her with those guys and . . . I don't know, I can't help getting this awful feeling that she's just tricking me."

"Dude, women are capable of anything," Benji said. "I told you that all along. You've got to know them to manage them properly. And, can I be honest?"

Josh nodded.

"It's your face," Benji said somberly. "That guy's looks like some Greek statue and yours is like a Halloween mask."

"Forget my face," Josh said. "You want to win this thing, right?"

"Of course," Benji said, "but I can't believe you kept this secret plan from me."

"So, what are we going to do?" Josh asked.

"You've got to tell your dad," Benji said.

"No," Josh said, whispering and hushing Benji with a finger to his lips. "I told you, it's a secret."

"But he could help," Benji said in a whisper.

"No, it would only make it worse," Josh said. He told Benji the deal about Myron's threat to Josh's father, humiliating him in the media and destroying his sponsorship with Nike. If the Titans lost, they'd still have a chance at another one-year sponsorship, but if his dad's credibility was destroyed, everything would be ruined.

"Why?" Benji asked.

"It just would," Josh said. "Stop asking."

"Okay then," Benji said, leaning close so Josh could hear him whisper. "Then there's only one thing we *can* do."

"What?" Josh asked.

CHAPTER FORTY-ONE

"GO SWIMMING," BENJI SAID.

"What?" Josh asked, rumpling his face in disbelief. "How's that going to help?"

"Hey, we've got until tomorrow night at this place," Benji said. "No way can we win if they got the umpire in their pocket, and no way we can stop it with Jaden working like some double agent, so we swim. We relax and just play—move on, like your mom says."

"Are you crazy?" Josh asked.

"No, I'm very sane, Josh. When you're beat, you're beat."

Josh shook his head and opened his book.

"Back to rabbits, huh?" Benji said. "I see."

"Rabbits who won't just quit," Josh said without looking up.

They didn't speak again until they were back at the camp. Josh returned his bat bag to the cabin, then told his parents he was heading into town. Benji emerged from the bathroom in his Red Sox cap and a big yellow bathing suit with blue fish all over it. In his hand was a bright green Nerf football.

"Let's hit the beach," Benji said, tugging on his cap.

Josh just turned and walked out the door, letting the screen door slam behind him. When Benji caught up, Josh didn't say anything.

"Come on," Benji said. "When we got off the bus, Esch told me his dad is grilling some sausages and peppers down by the water on one of those little grills. We can eat, swim, drink sodas. Come on, Josh, Carpet the D-end. Live a little."

Josh kept trudging and said, "*Carpe diem.* It's Latin. It means 'seize the day'—eat like a slob, drink soda until you're sick, lay around in the sun. Because, who cares? Tomorrow might never come.

"But it might come," Josh said, stopping and turning on Benji. "And if it does, I want to win that championship. I want us to walk away with that trophy because we're the best team and because my dad is the best coach. I know Mickey Mullen was a great baseball player, one of the greatest. I know he was way better than my dad. You should have seen the way that HBO producer looked at me when I said he was a pro player, like what he did in the minors was nothing, so my dad couldn't even *be* a rival to Mickey Mullen. But it wasn't nothing, and my dad is a better coach than Mickey Mullen—he's his rival there. Only my dad would never pay off an umpire just so he could win. I have a chance to stop that, maybe not much of a chance, but a chance. So you go stuff your face and flop around in the water, but I'm going into town. I'm like the rabbits. I'm not taking the easy way. I've got a dream, and I'm going to do everything I can to make it happen."

Benji's mouth fell open. "Gee, you're making me feel like a schmuck."

Josh shrugged and headed for the shuttle. When the bus coughed to life in a cloud of purple smoke, Josh ran to catch it. He hopped up the steps, ignored by the cranky driver.

"Oh no," she said suddenly. "Not on this bus. You get right off."

Josh spun around in surprise, only to see that the driver was talking to Benji, who climbed the steps in his yellow suit, Red Sox cap, and bare feet, wearing nothing else besides the Nerf ball he used to cover his jiggling belly button.

"My dad said he talked to you about us," Josh said.

"Right," she said. "You can ride, but not like *that*. Read the sign: 'No Bare Feet. Must Wear Shirt.' He's off."

"Wait," Benji said, "this is an emergency. We're like the rabbits in *Watership Down* trying to save their whole warren from a huge disaster. You gotta let me on, lady. This kid *needs* me."

The driver twisted up her face and shook her head. "You're nuts."

"How nuts is this?" Benji asked, removing his hat and showing the driver the Mickey Mullen signature on his cap. "Here, take it. You like Mickey Mullen?"

The driver's lower lip flopped open and trembled.

"This ain't real," she said.

"Met him at the museum the other day," Benji said with a wink. "All yours if you cut me a break."

The driver looked Benji up and down and sucked in her lower lip before she wagged her head toward the back.

"Deal," she said, swapping out her old Red Sox cap for the new one signed by Mickey Mullen.

Josh slid over to the window and Benji plunked down beside him with a huff.

"Benji, you didn't have to do that," Josh said quietly, feeling slightly guilty.

"You think I want that cheater's autograph messing up a good Red Sox hat?" Benji asked, raising an eyebrow. "Naw."

"You could have sold it," Josh said.

"Yeah," Benji said with a shrug. "I know."

"How much was that worth, anyway?"

"Not that much, really," Benji said. "Mickey Mullen must spend half his life signing autographs. I went online at the camp office and there's about ten thousand signed caps for sale on the internet."

"Ten thousand?"

"Without sweat stains," Benji said.

"Yours had a sweat stain?"

"I wore it to bed the other night, that hot one?" Benji said. "I think it was Wednesday. I couldn't get ten cents for that stupid thing."

Josh smiled and patted Benji's bare shoulder.

When they arrived at the drop-off in town, Benji asked, "So, what's the plan?"

They stepped off the bus and wandered down toward the marina. Josh couldn't help hoping he'd see Myron and Seevers at the restaurant again. He grew frustrated as Benji hopped along beside him, stepping gingerly on the grass, worried about getting a bee sting or stepping on glass in his bare feet. When they reached the parking lot, Benji stopped and stared.

"I'm not walking across that," Benji said. "It's like hot coals."

"I'll be right back," Josh said, crossing the lot and wandering through the restaurant to no avail. As he left, his cell phone rang.

It was Jaden.

CHAPTER FORTY-TWO

"CAN'T TALK," JADEN SAID in a hurried whisper, "but get to the Otesaga. By the pool."

Before Josh could say one word, the phone went dead. He looked around, then hurried outside to Benji.

"Jaden called."

"From where?" Benji said. "Did she helicopter all the way to California? Tell her to stay there."

"She said, 'Get to the Otesaga,'" Josh said. "And something about the pool."

"Here, let me call her back," Benji said, reaching for Josh's phone. "I'll tell her who can Otesaga and who can't."

"No, Benji," Josh said, snatching the phone back. "Use your own phone."

"I will," Benji said, pulling it free from his bathing suit pocket and holding it up.

"I thought you were going swimming?" Josh said.

"I take it out of my pocket when I go in," Benji said. "Dude, stop sounding like a mother hen."

"Otesaga means something," Josh said. "What?"

Benji shrugged, replacing his phone after all, and said, "Sounds Native American to me."

"It does," Josh said, "but what?"

Benji pointed. Across the street and down the block a ways was a small white building with a sign that said VISITOR INFORMATION.

"Good idea," Josh said.

"Uhh, would you mind?" Benji said, holding out his arms and wiggling his fingers.

"Mind what?"

"Carrying me?"

"Man, Benji," Josh said, looking him over. "You weigh half a ton and you're all sweaty, not to mention half naked."

Benji held up his foot and wiggled his toes. "You do not want these piggies to fry, dude. The Heavy Hitter needs to run free around the infield come tomorrow night. Come on. I gave up my Mickey Mullen Red Sox cap to help you. The least you could do is give me a little assistance."

"You said you didn't even want that hat," Josh said, "that it wasn't worth ten cents."

Benji folded his arms and looked away.

"Okay, come on," Josh said, "but you hang on to my

neck and ride on my back. I'm not carrying you across like you're some princess bride."

Josh backed up and Benji slung his arms around his neck. Josh carried his friend across the hot pavement and they went inside the information place, where Josh asked the woman if she had any idea what Otesaga was.

"Oh, it's a beautiful hotel just down the road," she said, pointing. "Right on the water. They have a golf course. Shirts required, of course."

Benji adjusted the Nerf ball to block his belly button.

"Do they have a pool?" Josh asked.

"A heated one," she said, nodding.

When they stepped out onto the sidewalk, Benji asked, "Can we get something to eat first? I could go for a bag of cheeseburgers, but even an ice cream could fill the gap a little bit."

"No," Josh said. "We've got to get to the Otesaga. Jaden made it sound urgent. I'm not missing this chance."

They walked up the street until they came to a light and had to cross again to get over the hot pavement to the lake side, where the road ran out from the center of town. Benji opened his arms and tilted his head. Josh didn't complain—he just carted him across and they headed up the sidewalk. The walked by several old mansions before they saw the Otesaga rise up above the trees in front of them. Soon the whole thing came into view. Sitting atop a grassy knoll with the lake glittering beyond, the Otesaga was enormous. It reminded Josh of a fortress.

The curving drive led to the covered entrance where massive three-story columns supported the eaves of a roof capped off with an enormous cupola. A man wearing a tan uniform trimmed in dark green stopped them to ask if they were guests of the hotel. Josh thought quick.

"Mickey Mullen Junior invited us," he said. "He said we should meet him by the pool."

The man straightened and said, "Oh. I saw their helicopter land just a few minutes ago over on the golf course. I heard they had to go down to New York City to pick up some movie stars for the big party tonight. How about that? Sure, go right on through. The pool is in the back."

Josh marched up the steps, with Benji following. They entered the elegant lobby, passing by the front desk with a wave and continuing on past the expensive furniture and straight out back to the circular deck.

"Well," Benji said, looking around uncomfortably, "we're here. Now what?"

"She had to have a reason," Josh said. "Maybe this is where they're doing it."

"Doing what?" Benji asked.

"Making the exchange," Josh said. "We need two

things. The first is a picture of Myron handing Seevers the envelope."

Josh looked around.

People passed them by in fancy summer clothes: men in slacks, women in flowery hats and high-heeled shoes. A long, sweeping row of rocking chairs sat facing the sloping lawn, the expanse of the lake, and the mountains beyond. On the terrace below, people sat having poolside drinks beneath an army of broad umbrellas shading them from the sun.

"Hey," Josh said, "I just realized: we'll need to use your cell. I don't have a camera on my phone. Jaden's got one, and I didn't think I'd have to do this without her."

"Forget a picture," Benji said, beaming and withdrawing the cell phone from his flouncy shorts. "You can shoot a video with this thing. Good thing you got me."

"Yeah, it is," Josh said, accepting the phone with a smile.

"There's the pool," Benji said, pointing. "Let's check it out. I feel like I stick out up here in the lobby with all these fancy-pants people."

"Nah," Josh said. "Those yellow swim trunks are great."

They descended the broad staircase, and as they did Josh examined the crowd beneath the umbrellas. Halfway down the steps, he froze and grabbed

Benji by the arm. In the shadow of an umbrella, sipping some kind of drink, Josh spotted Myron. Sitting across from him with a beer was Justin Seevers, the crooked umpire.

CHAPTER FORTY-THREE

JOSH GRABBED BENJI'S ARM and pointed. "There."

"How are we going to get a shot from here?" Benji asked.

"We've got to get closer," Josh said, scanning the area and descending the final steps until they stood on the terrace. "Here, come on."

Josh circled around the pool area. Surrounding the low rock wall was a hedge. Down near some trees, Josh looked around, then ducked into the narrow gap between the hedge and the wall, crawling on his hands and knees back around toward the table where he'd seen Myron and Seevers.

"Ow," Benji said behind him. "These bushes are biting into me."

"Shh," Josh said, twisting around to glare at him. "I'll go alone if you can't fit."

"I can *fit*," Benji said, hissing. "I've got sensitive skin is all. You don't want me itching all over when I'm swinging for the fences, do you?"

"Oh brother," Josh said, turning back around and continuing his crawl.

When they got to Myron's table, Josh peeked his head up over the wall, then ducked back down quickly.

"What's the matter?" Benji asked, bumping up behind him.

"I'm afraid they'll see me," Josh said, still whispering as he fumbled with the phone.

"Look," Benji said, pointing to the phone, "just hold it up and tilt the screen down. You can use it like a periscope."

Josh did as Benji said, and it was true: he could angle the phone so that by propping it just over the lip of the stone wall, he could see Myron and Seevers on the screen. After a while, though, his arm began to tremble with fatigue.

"I wish they'd just do it already," Josh said in a whisper.

"Want me to take a turn?" Benji said. "I'm just sitting here like one of those garden gnomes and my stomach is going crazy. I need a distraction."

"Okay," Josh said, "come closer and I'll just pass it off. Wait."

Josh froze. In the tiny cell phone screen he saw Myron reaching underneath the table. Josh pushed the button and started to record. Myron lifted the same kind of manila envelope he'd given Seevers before and handed it to him across the table. Seevers shook it and said something and the two of them laughed together as Seevers slipped the envelope under his arm and stood to go.

"I got it," Josh said, barely able to contain the excitement.

"Let me see," Benji said, groping.

"Don't break it, Benji," Josh said.

"Dude, it's my phone," Benji said. "Don't worry."

"I'm worried about what's on it," Josh said. "Not the phone."

"Nice," Benji said, snatching it away and fumbling with the buttons. "Let me see if you even got it. You may be the baseball great, but I'm a technology wizard. Oops."

"Oops?" Josh said. "What 'oops,' Benji?"

Benji held up a hand. "Can we get out of these bushes? Even a wizard needs decent working conditions."

"Go," Josh said. "I'll follow you."

Josh grumbled the entire length of the crawl, resisting the temptation of swatting Benji's big yellow butt as he waddled through the hedge. When they emerged into the shadows of the trees, Josh glanced over at the table where the exchange had taken place. Myron sat sipping his drink, staring at the activity in the pool with a small grin on his face.

"I don't know if you did this right," Benji said.

"I did it right," Josh said, growing hot. "*You're* the one who said 'oops.' I didn't say 'oops.' I saw him handing over the envelope and I hit the record button. Don't even tell me it's not on there, Benji."

Benji screwed up his face and poked the tip of his tongue out from the corner of his mouth as he fumbled with the phone keys.

"Yes!" he said, holding it up. "Saved the day."

"You ruined the day, then you saved it."

"Saved it all the same," he said.

"Let's see," Josh said.

Benji played the video, and Josh felt a surge of pride.

"I got it," he said, watching the video of Myron leaning over the table and handing Seevers the envelope.

"*We* got it," Benji said.

"We did. Now, send it to Jaden's phone to back it up."

"You said we needed two things," Benji said, frowning. "What's the other?"

CHAPTER FORTY-FOUR

SOMEONE CLEARED HER THROAT behind Josh and Benji and said, "Now we need the envelope."

Both boys spun around and spoke at the same time. "Jaden?"

"Who did you think?" she asked.

"Not Mickey Mullen Junior's *girl*friend," Benji said.

"Cut it out, Lido," Josh said.

"Dude, she rode in the guy's helicopter," Benji said.

"And gave us the heads-up on Myron's meeting with Seevers," Josh said.

He clasped Jaden by the shoulder and gave it a squeeze.

"Did you get it?" she asked.

Benji held up the phone with a nod. "Video. The whole thing. We just sent you a copy."

"You're big-time, Lido," Jaden said, slapping his back. "Come on, let's get out of here."

Jaden kept looking over her shoulder as if she expected someone to be following them. They darted between the trees and around the side of the massive hotel, winding through the landscaping, hurrying until they reached Lake Street.

"Okay," Benji said, tramping down the sidewalk toward town. "Now we've got to eat. You can't do this to me anymore. I am starved. This is cruel and unusual punishment."

Josh and Jaden hurried along behind Benji. Jaden took out her phone.

"Who are you calling?" Josh asked.

"My dad," she said. "I got to check in. I don't want him worrying."

"What are you going to say?" Josh asked, but Jaden's call had already gone through and she held up her finger.

"Dad?" she said. "Yeah, it was fun. Yeah, I met Anne Hathaway. She was nice. Um, Mickey invited me to this big barbecue they're having at the Otesaga. A bunch of celebrities are going to be there—Anne Hathaway and Orlando Bloom—you don't mind if I go, right?"

Jaden nodded her head, then said, "Thanks, Dad, you're the best."

Benji spun around. "Did you just say 'Anne Hathaway'?"

Jaden said, "I guess she and Orlando were in New York doing a movie or something and the Mick flew them in his jet. They're friends."

"Can *I* go to that thing?" Benji asked. "As *your* friend?"

"Now we're friends?" Jaden asked, forcing a smile. "Nice, Lido the fair-weather friend. Only I'm not going."

Benji's eyes widened. "You just told your dad. Now you're lying to your dad? Dude, you are so changed. That's classic Hollywood."

"I didn't lie, Benji," she said, stamping her foot. "Tell me how I lied."

"You said you're going to that barbecue," Benji said.

"No, I said they were having a barbecue and that I was invited, all true. I asked if he minded if I went. He said I could. I never said I *was*."

Benji slapped Josh's chest with the backs of his fingers and said, "You see what I was saying about women? Very dangerous."

Jaden hefted her phone at them and said, "You guys better do the same thing. It's starting to get late and you don't want your mom all worried and your dad hunting you down, right?"

Josh took out his own phone and pulled the same stunt with his mom as Jaden had with her dad, asking permission to go to the party at the Otesaga, saying Jaden had been invited and that she wanted them to hang out with her tonight. All true.

They entered town and found Benji the cheese-burgers he'd been craving, eating on the sidewalk outside the Triple Play Café as the sun dropped behind the buildings and the shadows grew long. After emp-tying a bag of two triple cheeseburgers, fries, and a milkshake, Benji suggested a pit stop at Esposito's Italian Ice Cream. Jaden and Josh both rolled their eyes.

"We've got to get going," Josh said. "You had your food."

"Besides," Jaden said. "You don't want to be too weighted down. What if we have to run?"

"Run?" Benji said, catching up with them at the door. "Why would we run? Where are we going?"

"You don't think Seevers is just going to give us that envelope filled with cash, do you?" Jaden asked, step-ping out onto the sidewalk. "We've got to go get it."

"Wait, can't the police get it?" Benji asked. "Or some other grown-ups or something? I didn't think you meant *us.*"

"Us," Jaden said, continuing to walk.

Josh nodded. "The police aren't going to do anything until we can prove they're paying off the umpire."

"Even then," Jaden said, "I don't think it's the police we go to. I think the only help we'll get is from the media. If we can prove it to them, it'll be a huge story. Then maybe someone will do something—the people at the Hall of Fame or the ones who run the tournament.

I don't know if what they're doing is criminal, but it's just really, really wrong. No, we've got to go there by ourselves."

"Where is 'there'?" Benji asked, his voice sounding small.

"Josh didn't tell you?" Jaden said. "Seevers's place."

CHAPTER FORTY-FIVE

BENJI CLEARED HIS THROAT and said, "Really, you guys, one of us should be at that barbecue in case either of your parents asks about it. I can go and give you guys a report. Look, it's gonna be dark soon and the mosquitoes will be out. I don't even have a shirt. I got no shoes."

"Come on," Jaden said, leading them down the street to Pioneer Alley, where they walked into a gift shop.

Benji watched in horror as Jaden removed a pair of pink rubber flip-flops from a plastic bin and placed them on the checkout counter along with a flimsy white T-shirt with SpongeBob wearing a Yankees cap on it. The total came to seven dollars and change. Jaden took the money from her pocket, paid, and handed the stuff to Benji.

"Shoes and a shirt," she said. "No more excuses. SpongeBob even matches your shorts."

"*Pink* sandals?" Benji asked.

"They're kind of cute," Jaden said.

Benji moaned but dropped them onto the sidewalk and slipped them on along with the T-shirt.

"Great," he said, his words as glum as his expression. "Anne Hathaway's at the Otesaga and I'm running around Cooperstown dressed like a Disneyland fairy."

Josh led his friends to the edge of town, where Seevers's place and other ancient homes backed up to the river. By the time they reached the gravel drive with its two small stone gateposts, the sun had disappeared behind the trees and the sky was fading to purple in the coming night. Heat still bled up from the pavement, but already the woods offered cool wafts of evening air.

"We're just going to walk right down the driveway?" Jaden asked.

"No reason to get all cut up or lost in the woods," Josh said. "If we see headlights coming, we'll have plenty of warning and we can hide in the trees."

They followed him along the winding drive where the overhang of trees made it quite dark and the gravel crunched beneath their feet. Jaden put a hand on Josh's shoulder, and Benji put his hand on the other one. A sudden clatter of sticks and a shriek made them all jump. Josh pulled himself together and said in a loud whisper, "It's just a bird, an owl or something."

"I know that," Benji said.

It wasn't long before gloomy yellow blotches of light appeared through the trees. The leaves flickered in a small breeze and the glow of the windows seemed to pulse with some inner heartbeat of the house, a monster crouching in the shadows. On the far side of the house, a window cast its beam on the low mound with its crumbling tombstones. The breeze carried with it the smell of the river's mud and something else, breath from the damp rot that ate away at the wooden house.

"Holy moly," Benji said, pointing. "Don't even tell me those are tombstones."

"Okay," Josh said, "I won't tell you."

"Because if some ax-murdering zombie comes blowing out of that house screaming at us," Benji said, "I'm the one who'll go down. Sure, the heavy kid in the pink flip-flops, he's the one who caught the ax blade in the back of the head. Poor kid, he never stood a chance. I can hear it on the news right now."

"There's no zombies," Josh said, annoyed at the feeling of fright that had curled up in the corner of his stomach like a rodent. "Just a weird, greedy, crooked umpire."

They crept forward, heading for the house. They walked along staring up into the lifeless windows. When they turned the corner at the rear of the house, they saw a flicker of light coming from a window that looked out onto the back porch. Josh crept up the steps, dodged past a couple of broken wicker chairs, and waved for them to join him at the window. Peering through the curtains, they saw Seevers slumped down on a couch in front of the TV, cradling a whisky bottle against the fur on his naked chest.

"Looks like he's out of it," Jaden whispered.

Josh nodded and led them back down the steps and around the other side of the house, where light spilled out from another window. When Josh got to the window, he reached up, grasped the sill, and did a chin-up so he could peek in.

"Holy moly," he said, peering through the screen. "There it is."

Jaden and Benji gripped the slimy windowsill with their fingertips and hoisted themselves up as well so they could peek over its edge. In a small room with a musty-looking double bed and a floor lamp with no shade, a battered desk faced the opposite wall next to the door. On the desk, beside a cluster of empty beer cans, rested the manila envelope with fat stacks of green bills spilling from its mouth.

"Yeah, but what do we do now?" Benji asked, his voice quavering.

CHAPTER FORTY-SIX

JOSH LET GO AND dropped to the ground.

"What are we going to do?" Jaden asked.

"We've got to think," Josh said. "We need a plan."

Benji and Jaden followed him and they huddled up behind the tree. Josh studied the house in silence as the evening deepened into night. Suddenly Benji pointed up at the peaks of the roof jutting into the early set of stars.

"Oh gosh," he said. "Look. Do you see?"

Josh narrowed his eyes and saw the flicker of wings, darting and dabbing around the edges of the roof.

"Bats," Benji said.

"Relax," Josh said. "They eat insects."

"And suck your blood," Benji said.

"That's vampire bats," Jaden said. "They're in South

America. You don't have anything to worry about. Stop being a pain."

"Bats have rabies," Benji said insistently as he inched away. "Rabies can kill you. You go mad and start foaming at the mouth. Then you're wracked with pain until you go stiff and just croak. I saw it in a movie."

"Lido," Josh said, yanking him back. "We're not leaving. You want to go, you go ahead, but I'm not going without that envelope. We're supposed to play for the national championship tomorrow night, and I'm not going to let this creep ruin it for us."

"Well," Benji said, "we're just sitting here. It's not going to fly out the window at us."

"Okay," Josh said, making up his mind. "Cell phones out, everyone. Jaden, you can conference with yours, right?"

"Yeah," she said.

"So, you tie us all in together," Josh said. "Everybody put their phone on vibrate first."

They did, and Jaden then linked them all onto the same call.

"Good," Josh said, sneaking a look at the big, gloomy house. "Okay, now look around for a piece of metal or something. I need something to help me pry that screen off."

They fished around in the grass, and near the house Jaden came up with an old metal bracket.

"Good," Josh said, hefting the rusty metal. "Okay,

after you guys help me through the window, Benji, you watch the front door. Jaden, you watch the back. If either of you sees anything, you let me know on the phone."

"This is, like, breaking and entering," Jaden said in a low whisper as they stepped up beneath the window. "Then we take the money? We could go to jail."

"We're not stealing it," Josh said, looking up at the sagging screen. "We're investigating corruption. Stealing is when you take something and you plan on keeping it. That's not what we're doing. We're going to borrow it to show the people who run the tournament that it's the same envelope Myron gave to Seevers. If they don't believe the video, their fingerprints are all over that thing. Now, you guys boost me up."

"What about Seevers?" Jaden asked, nodding her head toward the back of the big old house.

"He's half in the bag," Josh said in a whisper. "If the roof fell on him, he wouldn't notice, but if he does get up, one of you will see him and we'll all run like heck."

Benji looked up at the window, shook his head, and said, "This is bad. This is so bad."

"Bad is what they're doing," Josh said. "Robbing kids of a chance to win a championship, or my dad the chance for a long-term sponsorship. That's bad. That's stealing, not this. Hurry up and help me here."

Jaden and Benji each cupped their hands together and bent down so Josh could step into them. Then they raised him up so that he could pry the screen loose, drop the bracket down into the grass, and slither inside. He slipped and thumped to the bedroom floor, dizzy with fear for a moment before he scrambled up and gave them a thumbs-up, pointing to his phone, then silently directing each of them toward the front and back of the house.

He watched them disappear, then turned back into the room.

The light next to the bed cast a yellow glow over musty sheets and stained pillows. Josh moved carefully toward the dresser where he'd seen the envelope of money.

He was only halfway there when Benji screamed.

CHAPTER FORTY-SEVEN

JOSH BOLTED TO THE dresser, grabbed, and felt the envelope in his fingers. He spun, leaped across the room,
threw the envelope out the window and into the night,
then quickly scrambled out of the window himself before
falling in a heap on the grass.

"What happened?" Josh asked in a frightened hiss
as he got to his feet.

Benji ran toward him from the front, swatting the air
over his head. Then he tripped and fell to the ground,
still screaming. The bat that had swooped down and
fluttered about his head zigzagged off into the trees.

"Benji, it's gone," Josh said, grabbing two handfuls of
Benji's SpongeBob T-shirt and hauling him to his feet.

"What happened?" Jaden said, hissing as she
appeared from the back.

"Benji got attacked by a bat," Josh said, also in an urgent whisper.

Jaden looked down, scooped up the envelope from the grass, and said, "Let's get the heck out of here."

Benji yelped again, and Josh scowled at him in disgust.

"I told you," Josh said, looking around above Benji's head, "the bat's gone. Be *quiet*."

Benji's face had gone white, and it glowed at them in the darkness like a pale moon. He raised a finger, pointing behind them, past the graveyard and toward the front of the house.

"It's him," Benji said, trembling.

Josh spun around and gasped. Seevers stood there, bare-chested and wearing nothing but a pair of blue-and-white-striped pajama bottoms with his frizzy gray hair sticking up like a maniac. That's not what made Josh gasp, though.

The umpire was carrying a shotgun.

His mouth barely moved as he said, "You kids don't move. Not a muscle."

CHAPTER FORTY-EIGHT

"RUN!" JADEN SCREAMED.

Josh didn't think, he jumped, and when his feet hit
the ground they took off like three jackrabbits running
for cover. The blast of the shotgun only made him run
faster. He felt the hot rush of pellets swooshing overhead
and hissing on through the night. He glanced left and
right as he tore through the trees and down the grassy
lawn, following Jaden and seeing Benji over his left
shoulder moving like he'd never seen him move before.

All three of them careened down the hill toward the
river. Their momentum and their instincts carried them,
running straight away from the house and the dark
woods and the graveyard and the crazy umpire with the
shotgun. But when they reached the dock, they clustered
together in the shadow of the slat-board boathouse.

Josh peered around the corner, his hands on the trim and breaking off flakes of paint brittle with age.

"Is he coming?" Benji asked. "What do we do? Swim?"

"He is coming," Josh said, terror clutching his insides, "but he's moving slow."

Josh turned, forced open the door, and stepped into the boathouse, which smelled of dead fish and tar. The moon in the open sky above the river shed enough light through the wide opening for them to see.

Josh pointed and said, "There's a boat."

Actually there were two boats, a small aluminum rowboat with an outboard motor in the nearest slip and a long, thin wedge of a speedboat with fat chrome pipes suspended in a lift above the water of the second slip.

"Are you nuts?" Benji said. "This guy's trying to kill us. He *shot* at us."

"So, we've got nothing to lose," Josh said, crouching down beside the nearest slip and loosening the lines that held the small motorboat in place. "Come on."

Jaden hopped down into the boat, and its aluminum side clanged against the pier. As Benji scrambled in, the boat tipped and Jaden almost toppled over the side.

"Easy!" she said, but Benji paid no attention as he fiddled with the motor.

Josh ducked back outside and peeked around the corner. The ump was halfway down the lawn, coming along, slow but steady, the shotgun nestled in his arms. Josh darted back inside, slammed the door shut, then leaped into the boat. Benji pulled the cord, but the ancient motor only sputtered. Jaden threw up her hands and turned to Josh with a look of exasperation and fear.

"Benji," Josh said, "yank that thing with all your might."

Benji tottered but gripped the rubber handle and pulled the cord hard. The motor sputtered, then died.

Outside, the old guy shouted, "You thieves! I'll kill you!"

A shotgun blast roared and a spray of pellets thrashed the side of the boathouse. Benji flew into the bottom of the boat.

"Oh no," Benji whined, squirming. "I'm hit. I'm swimming in my own blood."

Josh hauled him up and said, "It's motor oil. He hit the wall. Get us out of here!"

Benji turned and yanked the cord again.

They heard the thump of the old guy's footsteps outside on the dock and the distinctive clatter of a fresh round being pumped into the shotgun's chamber.

The motor sputtered and coughed.

Benji hammered the choke lever, up and down.

Blue smoke erupted from the motor.

The door kicked open.

The motor caught and roared to life.

CHAPTER FORTY-NINE

BENJI FUMBLED WITH THE controls. Josh shoved him aside, taking over and slamming the outboard into reverse. The boat lurched backward. Jaden spilled over the seat and fell, her arms pinwheeling. Benji grabbed the back of her collar and tugged hard, keeping her from going over the edge while the boat shot backward out into the river. They swerved back and forth, rocking wildly, but Josh kept the boat moving and heading away from the crazy old guy with his shotgun.

Jaden gripped the boat's sides and steadied herself in the bottom beside Benji. Josh looked back at the shrinking shape of the boathouse and saw the sudden flash of orange light in the mouth of its dark opening. The shotgun blast followed it an instant later, as did the eruption of water off the starboard side of the motorboat.

Josh swerved suddenly, backing around but nearly tipping the boat. He glanced down at Jaden, then slammed the gear lever into forward. It clanked and roared and they took off like a rocket, down the narrow river outlet and out toward the lake. When they reached the open water, even though the boathouse had already disappeared from sight, Josh kept going. The moon had ducked behind some clouds, and he drove straight for the empty darkness in the middle of the lake for another five or ten minutes before he slowed the boat and let the motor idle.

"Is everyone okay?" he asked.

"Only thanks to my extra padding that broke the fall," Benji said, smacking his backside.

They all laughed and realized that while none of them was hurt, they were all trembling.

"You should have seen your face," Josh said to Benji.

"You should have seen yours, dude," Benji said.

Josh pointed at Benji's yellow bathing suit and said, "Dude, did you pee your pants?"

Benji looked down, and even in the weak light of the stars his face clearly went red as he slapped at his suit.

"I got splashed by motor oil," Benji said. "You know I did!"

"I don't know anything," Josh said, teasing.

"Dude, you so do."

"I know," Josh said, patting Benji on the back as he turned his attention to Jaden and the envelope she held clutched to her chest. "Well, we got the proof. What now?"

"Let's get this thing into the marina and get the shuttle bus back to the camp," Jaden said, pointing toward the lights of town. "Bob Costas gave me his card when I met him the other night. If someone big like him breaks this story, the rest will take care of itself."

Jaden's face grew somber. "Once we do, though, they'll know it was us who took the money. Technically, we broke into that guy's house."

"And technically," Josh said, "he tried to kill us."

"There was nothing technical about it," Benji said. "He flat-out tried."

"Maybe he was shooting over our heads," Jaden said. "Either way, everything that happened back there is gonna be a wash. He's not going to press charges if we don't."

"That guy should be locked up!" Benji said, his voice cracking.

"Relax," Josh said. "Jaden's right. Let's go for the wash. We don't need any trouble either."

The distant drone of an engine buzzed toward them like a wasp caught in a curtain.

Josh froze. "Hey, what's that?"

They all looked back in the direction they'd come from.

Surging up out of the mouth of the river was another

set of lights, one red and one white—the lights of a boat. In seconds it became a roar, and Josh remembered the boat with the chrome pipes suspended in the boathouse. The piercing scream of the speedboat's chrome pipes were the source of the noise. A sharp beam of white light burst suddenly from the nose of the speedboat and swept back and forth across the lake's rippled surface, heading their way.

"Hurry!" Jaden shouted above the scream of the speedboat. "He gets us in that light and we'll never get away!"

CHAPTER FIFTY

JADEN POINTED TOWARD THE marina and shouted, "Go!"

Josh opened the throttle as wide as it would go, willing the small boat to move faster. He scowled at the spray the bow plowed up in front of them, then grabbed Benji by the collar and tugged him toward the stern, allowing the nose to rise higher above the water's surface so the boat could go even faster. Wind whipped their ears and the lake slapped the metal skin of the boat.

Jaden shouted for Josh to hurry, pointing back at the lights of the speedboat, racing toward them and closing a lot of distance.

The lights of town and the marina grew closer, but not fast enough.

"Hurry!" Benji yelled.

"I'm going as fast as I can!" Josh shouted.

"He's going to get us!"

The white light darted across the water, close enough now for Josh to see the storm of bugs in its beam. The rodent of fear in his stomach morphed into a snarling pit bull and he thought he'd be sick. When the light hit them it blinded Josh, and he automatically fell into the bottom of the boat, plastering his arm across his face to shield his eyes, crying out in pain and shock. Unmanned, their boat swerved. Josh heard the distinct earsplitting pipes of the speedboat. He peeked out from under his arm to see the speedboat taking a new angle, one that would cut them off from the marina.

When their boat lurched again, Josh was shocked to see that Jaden had gotten behind him and grabbed the controls. But, instead of heading for town, she was going directly for the Otesaga.

All Josh's fears and suspicions came back to him in a gush. He blinked in confusion and horror. He couldn't make sense of it. Why would Jaden take them right into the thick of the Mullens? They needed to get as far away from Myron and Mickey and his entourage as possible, but here she was, going straight for them and their big barbecue.

Above the noise he yelled, "What the heck are you doing?"

CHAPTER FIFTY-ONE

OUT ON THE HOTEL'S sloping back lawn, hundreds of people sat at rows of tables under the flickering glow of oil lamps on posts stuck into the grass. The grand hotel rose up in the background, muting the star-filled night with row after row of twinkling windows. The closer their boat got, the more people rose up out of their seats and migrated toward the shore as if drawn to the incoming beam from the spotlight like a colony of half-human moths.

Above the seating area, on a small stage, Mickey Mullen stood in an open collar shirt and jeans, holding a microphone.

"What are you doing!" Josh bellowed again, grabbing Jaden by the shoulder only to be swatted away. "We'll crash!"

Jaden's mouth seemed frozen in a maniacal grin, her teeth flashing in the beam of light. Josh yelled for Benji to hang on as he gripped the sides of the boat himself. No sooner did he have a hold than they ground up onto the stony beach with a screech of metal. The impact jarred his spine, and his teeth clacked. Finally they jerked to a halt. Just off the shore, the earsplitting speedboat roared in after them. At the last instant it cut the white light, swung about, and rocketed back out onto the empty lake, leaving a three-foot wave in its wake.

Before Josh could say anything, Jaden jumped out of the boat and raced up the hill toward the stage with the envelope in her hand. Josh followed, with Benji close behind. As Jaden neared the steps to the stage, Myron's apelike figure appeared from the gloom of the lawn above. In his hand was a cell phone. He shouted into it as he pointed toward Jaden.

Josh stumbled, unable to believe what he saw.

Myron reached out for the envelope and said, "Good job, Jaden. I'll take that."

CHAPTER FIFTY-TWO

JADEN LOOKED AT MYRON and said, "Oh no you won't."

She clutched the envelope and stepped back. Benji bumped into Josh and Josh into Jaden. He put his arm in front of her, stepping between her and Myron.

"Leave her alone," Josh said.

"You stole this!" Myron shouted.

Josh felt Myron's other hand grip him by the collarbone and probe beneath the bone for a jujitsu pressure point. Josh saw stars when Myron hit the nerve and he crumpled to the grass, paralyzed with pain. Myron ripped the envelope from Jaden's hands.

As Josh's eyes adjusted and he struggled to get up, he saw Benji grab a plastic bottle of something off the nearest table and run toward Myron.

"Have some hot sauce, Myron!" Benji shouted,

squirting the fiery red liquid into Myron's face.

Myron screamed and pawed at his eyes, dropping the envelope, spinning and tripping and going down hard on the grass. Jaden grabbed the envelope and leaped over Myron. She sprinted to the stage, landing on the third stair and continuing on up the stage and into the floodlights around the podium. Josh skirted around Myron and followed. Benji stayed behind to blast Myron's face with another dose of red-hot sauce. Myron screamed so loud that Mickey Mullen's jaw dropped.

Jaden snatched the microphone from Mickey and, before he could react, retreated behind Josh, using him as a shield. Then she turned to the crowd that now gawked up at the stage.

"I have to tell everyone that this is the money Mickey Mullen gave to the umpire of tomorrow's championship game!" she shouted, holding the envelope up high for everyone to see. "We've got a video, too, of Myron Underwood handing the cash to Justin Seevers, the umpire. We can prove it!"

The crowd murmured in shock.

Mickey Mullen stepped forward and took hold of the envelope. Jaden dropped the microphone and tried to hang on, but the Mick yanked it free. He hadn't taken another step before Josh got a grip on it, though. Josh and Mickey Mullen tugged back and forth until the envelope tore and stacks of money spilled to the stage. Josh knelt and grabbed a stack, only to have Mickey

Mullen step on his hand, pinning it to the floor. When Bob Costas rose from his seat at a table in front and stepped up onto the stage, Josh felt as if he'd been in a dream.

"That's it," Bob Costas said, holding up his hands. "Let him go or you'll all be front-page news."

Josh watched, fascinated, as Mickey Mullen's snarl transformed into a slick, toothy smile.

CHAPTER FIFTY-THREE

"OF COURSE I'LL LET him go," Mickey Mullen said, lifting his foot and broadening his smile before he picked up the microphone and spoke to the crowd. "This is an outrage, and I want to know what happened as much as anyone else."

"Jaden," Bob Costas said, "can I see the video you're talking about?"

Jaden stepped forward, punched up the video, then held out her cell phone as she asked, "If you write a story, can I help?"

"Sure," Bob Costas said.

"Please," Mickey Mullen said politely, speaking into the microphone as he looked over Bob Costas's shoulder. "I had no idea about any of this. If it's true, then Myron Underwood is finished."

Josh got to his feet as Bob Costas looked up from the video and said to Mickey Mullen, "It looks pretty clear that your man tried to fix the championship game."

"Unbelievable," Mickey Mullen said, shaking his head sadly. "It's despicable, but we stopped it, thank goodness."

Bob Costas studied the actor's face before nodding slowly. "Yeah, thank goodness."

"I think this girl deserves a reward," Mickey Mullen said into the microphone, appealing to the crowd. "What do you think, everyone? How about a college scholarship from the Mickey Mullen Foundation for Kids for the young lady who preserved the integrity of this great event?"

People cheered, and Mickey Mullen nodded with satisfaction, directing his grin now at Jaden and Josh. Benji appeared with a rib in one hand, licking the other free from hot sauce.

"Man," Benji said, "this stuff is smokin'. I think it's got chili peppers in it."

"Where's Myron?" Josh asked.

Benji jerked his head in the direction of the hotel. "He took off, but I don't think he's getting very far."

Josh heard an enormous splash from the direction of the pool.

"One way to rinse the hot sauce out of your eyes," Benji said, biting into the rib.

"Mickey," Bob Costas said in a low tone that Josh could barely hear, "why would your guy have done this?"

Mickey stood with his mouth open for a minute, and Josh could practically see the wheels turning in his brain before he leaned toward Bob Costas's ear and said, "He wanted a part in my next movie. He was desperate to be an actor. Really desperate. When I told him I didn't think it could happen, he gave me this funny smile and said he had some information that he knew would make me change my mind. I hate to say it, Bob, but now I see the guy was obviously going to blackmail me into getting a part."

Bob Costas studied the baseball legend for a few moments, then cleared his throat and, nodding slowly, said, "I think I understand."

Then he turned and walked off the stage. Josh and his friends caught up to the announcer as he ascended the grassy lawn toward the hotel.

"Mr. Costas," Josh said, "you don't believe him, do you?"

Bob Costas stopped and gave Josh the same thoughtful stare he'd given to Mickey Mullen. Finally he shook his head and said, "No, I don't."

"Then we'll write the story?" Jaden asked.

"No," Bob Costas said, "I don't think we will, Jaden."

"But you *have* to," Josh said. "You have to expose

him for the phony cheating rat that he is."

"I know how you feel," Bob Costas said, "but he's got a pretty tight story that explains all this away. As much as I'd like to take a cheater down, a good reporter won't go out with a story unless he or she is a hundred percent certain."

Josh hung his head.

"But don't worry," Bob Costas said, patting Josh on the shoulder, "most times guys like him get it in the end. Trust me, you can't do things like that forever without getting caught up in your own lies sooner or later. And when he does, maybe Jaden and I can write that story together. Now, if you'll excuse me, I've got a radio show I need to get to. Good luck to you guys tomorrow. I'll be there."

They watched the announcer continue on toward the hotel.

"At least you got a scholarship out of it," Josh said in a mutter to Jaden.

"Ha!" Benji said, tossing the chewed-up rib bone over his shoulder. "Fat chance of that. I bet your scholarship goes the way of my Mickey Mullen ice-cream cone. All talk."

"Did I hear my name?"

They turned to see Mickey Mullen standing there in the grass, talking heatedly to his PR lady, Ms. Simmons. Josh could only glare at them.

"Doesn't matter, really," Mickey Mullen said,

lowering his voice. "You chumps are still going to finish second tomorrow, umpire or no umpire. Now, get out of here before I call hotel security. This is a private party."

CHAPTER FIFTY-FOUR

WHEN JOSH'S PARENTS ASKED them about the party, they told half the truth and nothing but half the truth. They'd all decided on the shuttle bus back to the camp that mentioning the shotgun blasts would create more trouble than any of them wanted. Still, even without certain details, they were able to tell a convincing enough tale about the video, the money, and Mickey Mullen's accusation of Myron onstage so that Josh's parents were nearly as certain as they were that Mickey Mullen himself had tried to fix the game.

"Incredible," Josh's dad said, shaking his head, his mouth agog in disbelief. "Why didn't you tell me about all this sooner, Josh?"

Josh shifted uncomfortably in the little wooden chair that sat facing the musty couch in the cabin's small living room. He looked down at his feet and shrugged.

"There must have been a reason," his dad said, his voice rumbling in a way that let Josh know he had better give a good answer.

"Well," Josh said. "Right from the start, that Myron said he'd ruin you, Dad. He talked about how Mickey Mullen had the media eating out of his hand and said that if I opened my mouth, they'd get them to do a big story on you and make you look really bad."

Josh's dad shook his head. "I don't care how the media makes me out, Josh."

Josh kept his head down. Quietly he said, "They were going to talk about how you never made it, Dad. They said bad things. I know all that bothers you."

Josh glanced up to see his dad give his mom a weak smile and take her hand in his own giant paw.

"Your dad played thirteen years as a pro," his mom said softly. "Yeah, he never made it to the big leagues, but there're some guys in the big leagues who only play a year or two, and how do you think they feel? They wish they had more. People talk about athletes who are winners? Someone who does his best, goes as far as he can, and isn't ashamed or frightened of the things he *didn't* do? That's a winner."

Josh looked up. This time he nodded.

"And," Benji said somberly from his rocking chair in the corner of the room, "it's all about scoring, because the team who scores the most points *always* wins."

"Oh brother," Josh said.

"Don't forget what your mom said when you're playing tomorrow, Josh," his dad said, ignoring Benji. "You play your best. Enjoy being there. It's a huge accomplishment just to get to Cooperstown—think of what you had to go through with your eye, that surgery—and we have a great team. If we lose, then that's what was meant to be. Just do your best."

His mom and dad traded looks. Then his dad patted his mom on the leg. "Come on, Laura, let's go take a walk. Josh can listen for the baby if she gets up, right, Josh?"

"Sure," he said, "you guys go."

Josh watched them leave, clasping hands as they walked down the porch steps and out under the starry sky.

"How about a couple sodas?" Benji asked. "Hey, why the gloomy face?"

"Just thinking about what he said," Josh said.

"Yeah," Benji said, "your dad's a sharp cookie. Whatever's meant to be, right? We just let it happen and enjoy the whole thing. I love that."

"No," Josh said, "he's not right. Not about that. We can't just let it happen, Benji. We've *got* to win this thing tomorrow, and I'm not talking about winning it for us. I can't let Mickey Mullen think that he gets whatever he wants, like he's acting in some movie and we're all just a bunch of extras. We've *got* to win this thing.

"We've got to win it for my dad."

CHAPTER FIFTY-FIVE

THE CHAMPIONSHIP GAME TOOK place on the main field in the center of Dream Park. The Titans' bus dropped them off outside a battered green door in the side of the cinder-block field house where they were allowing the semifinalists to change and prepare. The locker room smelled like damp socks and dried mud. Josh examined his face in the mottled mirror and traced the scar beneath his eye as he pondered his mother's words from the night before.

"You ready?" Benji asked, patting him on the back.

Josh washed his hands and nodded without speaking.

Josh's dad called them together, speaking in his soft rumbling-thunder voice.

"Okay," he said, looking around at each of them,

246

"everyone knows by now that the Mick tried to buy off the umpire—or we think he did, anyway—but that's over. Don't lose your focus. The Mullen kid is still going to be the best pitcher we've seen. He throws more heat than anyone, but he's not perfect and I know a way we can beat him."

Josh shifted and looked around. The rest of the team stared at his father as if they were in a trance. He could tell they all believed in his dad, and Josh did too.

"He throws heat, but he's a little on the wild side," his dad said. "That's how we beat him, with our brains. We make him throw more pitches than he wants. First of all, he's pitched two entire games already this week, which is a lot. Second, the games he's pitched, the ump was giving him one heck of a big strike zone. After everything that's happened and everyone talking, that won't happen with the ump we'll get today.

"So, we wear him out. We make him throw eight to ten pitches for every batter. Don't worry about hitting it early on, just guard the plate. Get a piece of the ball— a foul is going to be like gold for us. It might not seem like it, but by the end, we'll have him worn out, and if I know Mickey Mullen, the dad, he's not going to pull his kid out, even if he's struggling. Trust me, guys. Hang in, protect the plate, and we'll get them in the end."

After a crisp cheer led by Josh's dad, they burst out of the locker room and took the field. Wind snapped at the pennants atop the stadium's flagpoles, and sunshine spilled down through a high haze of fish scale clouds. A hint of popcorn and cotton candy floated on the breeze along with the buzz of the growing crowd in the stands. The sight of TV cameras up in the top row of the bleachers and behind home plate made Josh's stomach roll. Jaden, her dad, and Josh's mom sat right behind the Titans dugout, and they all offered him a thumbs-up. Josh refused to look at Mickey Mullen or Mickey Jr. Instead, he lost himself in the pregame ritual of their pepper drill and warm-up swings.

With his hat over his heart, Josh felt a thrill as he heard "The Star-Spangled Banner." When the music ended, he pulled his cap on tight and turned to Benji. "This is it. Can you believe it? Everything we went through, and now we're really here."

"And they're here too," Benji said, pointing up to a section in the crowd where more than a dozen college coaches sat clustered together to scout the talent.

"Let's do it, Benji," Josh said, holding out a fist for Benji to bump. "We got an even field. No cheating. No tricks. Just baseball."

The mayor of Cooperstown stepped out to the pitcher's mound and announced the beginning of the first-ever Hall of Fame national championship game. The crowd cheered and the Titans did too as they dashed out onto the field. Josh planted his heels on the lip of grass between second and third, then rocked forward with his toes in the dirt, bent over and ready for anything.

Anything was what he got. The Comets could hit, and they kept the Titans busy in the field. Even with stellar defense that included two double plays through five and a half innings, the Titans found themselves down 5–3 going into the bottom of the final inning. Mickey Jr. had given up just four hits: a single to Esch and a home run to Josh in the first, along with a double by Josh in the third that sent a runner in to score before Mickey Jr. closed out the inning. The only bright side going into their last at bat was that the Titans were at the top of their order.

Josh's dad called the team together. Jaden had moved into the dugout with her pen and pad, and she took notes as Josh's father spoke.

"Okay, this is it," he said, kneeling down in front of them as they clustered together in the dugout. "This is right where we said we'd be. We can do it, but you've got to believe. Don't let Mullen intimidate you. He's not the same pitcher he was in the first inning. Trust me, his arm is going. He's worn out. I know he's only given up four hits, but even when we've struck out, we made him throw more pitches than is good for him. You did your job up until now—now we finish this thing. First three guys get on base. Josh, you clean it up. Okay, bring it in. 'Believe' on three. One, two, three—"

"BELIEVE!"

CHAPTER FIFTY-SIX

ESCH WAS THEIR LEADOFF batter, and the first two pitches Mickey Jr. threw had so much heat that Esch could only blink as they burned right by him down the middle. Esch stepped back out of the box with an 0–2 count and looked over at Josh's dad. His dad held up a clenched fist and nodded for him to hang in. Esch took a deep breath and stepped up. The next two pitches went wild. When the third pitch went just high and inside, Mickey Mullen shot out of the Comets dugout screaming at the umpire when he called it a ball.

The umpire was a huge man with a thick bull neck. The rumor around the park was that he was a college umpire the tournament had brought up from New York City. The ump held up his meaty hands as he warned Mickey Mullen that another tirade would be his last.

Esch stepped back into the box. The 3–2 pitch came, right down the middle. Esch swung over it but managed to nick it just enough so that it dribbled down the third-base line. The catcher threw off his mask and scrambled for it.

Esch took off like a shot and made it safely just as the catcher's throw made it to first.

"Good thing they don't own the ump," Jaden muttered to Josh after the cheering in their dugout subsided.

The next Titans batter went down but it took Mickey Jr. eleven pitches to do it, and Josh could see that his dad was right. The balls didn't have the heat they had before—far from it. The batter before Josh got up and hit a single over the shortstop's head, putting two on base with just one out.

Josh cheered from the batter's circle, then puffed out his cheeks and blew a gust of air. Jaden and Benji both gave him a thumbs-up. His dad stepped out of the dugout to slap him on the back and tell him to swing big. Josh nodded, then walked up to the plate and planted his feet in the batter's box.

That's when Mickey Mullen, the dad, jogged out to the mound.

CHAPTER FIFTY-SEVEN

THE FATHER AND SON talked back and forth at the bottom of the mound. Mickey's cheeks seemed to pinch at his eyes as he spat out a tirade of angry words at his son that Josh couldn't quite make out. Mickey Jr. didn't slouch—he stood tall and looked evenly at his famous father and shook his head no. Mickey Mullen's face went red and Josh heard the words, "You'll walk him if I tell you to walk him or you'll walk home to California."

The father turned and stomped back to the dugout. Mickey Jr. climbed the mound.

Josh stared out at Mickey Jr. and saw something that surprised him.

Mickey Jr. held his head high with defiance.

Josh set his feet, gritted his teeth, and cranked back his bat, ready for the pitch.

Mickey Jr. wound up, and when the ball left his hand, Josh knew it was a changeup. He read it perfectly, right down the middle, and swung with everything he had.

It was too much. Josh pulled the ball well outside the third-base line. It cleared the fence by a mile but was obviously foul.

"No," Mickey Mullen screamed from the dugout. "Don't you do it!"

The umpire tossed out a fresh ball. Mickey Jr. adjusted it in his glove and bit his lip. Glaring down at Josh, he wound up and threw another pitch down the middle with all the heat he could muster.

It was a fastball that wasn't so fast.

Josh got all of it and the ball took off, clearing the fence by more than a hundred feet. The crowd exploded, and as Josh circled the bases he couldn't help noticing Mickey Jr.'s chin hit his chest, and he couldn't help feeling bad for the opposing pitcher, knowing his famous father would be enraged with him for going against his wishes and failing.

To his credit, Mickey Mullen shook his head, clapped his hands at his son, and shouted for him to forget about it. The father shouted that if Mickey Jr. put down two more batters, the inning would be over—they could take it into extra innings and win it anyway.

Mickey Jr. took heart. He put the next Titans batter down with just four pitches, the last one a fastball that showed some life. All eyes in the stadium went to the

Titans batter's circle, where Benji stood with his jaw hanging slack.

Josh put a hand on Benji's arm, and his dad put his hand on the other. Benji trembled and gulped like a fish in the bottom of a boat.

"Hey," Josh said, "Batman and Robin. Heavy Hitter, right? That's you. You can do this."

"Benji," Josh's dad said, leaning over so he was eye level with Josh's best friend, "I know why you call yourself a heavy hitter all the time. I know you don't really believe that about yourself, but that's okay, because every good ballplayer grows up. They take the step between being a kid and a young man. It happens. Sometimes it happens when no one's looking. For you, it's gonna happen right here, right now, with all these people watching and with thousands of others checking you out on TV."

"Don't you mean millions?" Benji asked with a weak smile.

"It's ESPN Four," Josh's dad said, grinning, "don't get that excited. This is it, though. Trust me, Benji. His arm is worn down and you're putting this out of the park."

"Good luck, buddy," Josh said.

Benji staggered toward the plate, muttering to himself.

"What's he saying?" Josh's dad asked him.

"He's saying 'heavy hitter,' Dad," Josh said, then he crossed his fingers for luck.

Benji dusted off his hands and spit into his glove. He held up one hand and stepped into the batter's box. The first pitch came fast and inside. Benji swung for the fences and fouled it off the handle of his bat.

"You're making contact!" Josh's dad shouted.

"Get him, Benji!" Jaden shouted.

Josh bit his lip.

The next pitch came fast down the middle. Benji swung so hard he spun himself into the dirt. The ball smacked the catcher's mitt and the catcher tossed it back to Mickey Jr., who fought back a smile.

"Oh brother," Jaden said, moaning to Josh and clenching his arm in her grip, "an 0–2 count."

"Believe," Josh said in a whisper.

Mickey Jr. looked at his dad, who signaled something. Then he took a deep breath, wound up, and threw a fastball too high to be a strike.

Benji reared back and swung.

CHAPTER FIFTY-EIGHT

JOSH FELT THE MOAN escape him. But Benji, off balance and reaching for the sky with his bat, connected.

CRACK.

The ball took off like an airplane, climbing higher as it went, arcing over the right fielder's head and dropping toward the fence. Benji took off.

Everyone screamed.

When the ball hit the fence with a clang, Josh felt Jaden's fingers dig straight down to his bone. The ball popped up and fell, and none of them could tell if it was inside or outside the fence.

Benji ran for all he was worth, his foot smacking the second-base bag. The right fielder sprinted toward the fence, reaching for the ball like it was still in play. Benji was halfway to third with his back to the outfielder and already slowing down, extending his arms to receive the cheers of the crowd.

The outfielder threw his shoulder into the fence and reached down, springing back out onto the grass with the recoil of the metal mesh and cranking back his arm to make a throw.

Benji rounded third and—even though he'd disavowed the player after his steroid use—tipped off his batting helmet like Manny Ramirez, arms still out, loving the applause and hamming it up for the TV cameras.

Josh and his dad and the entire Titans team screamed for Benji to run. Benji turned his head and saw the right fielder launch the ball. His face dropped in complete shock, but instead of freezing, Benji clenched his jaw and took off. He put his head down, churning forward, fighting for top speed to beat the throw.

Jaden chewed on a knuckle and said, "He'll never make it."

CHAPTER FIFTY-NINE

THE BALL HIT THE grass just inside the infield dirt and bounced toward home plate. The catcher had to step to his left, a few feet up the baseline. Benji and the ball raced for the same spot.

The catcher caught the ball on a bounce with a smack, pinning it with both hands into the pocket of the mitt and turning to tag Benji.

Benji's face contorted with momentary horror, then he snarled and dipped his shoulder and plowed straight through the catcher. His shoulder caught the catcher in the chest and he drove upward. The catcher flew into the air, twisting as he fell. Benji lost his balance and fell forward, his hands smacking home plate. The catcher landed with a thud, his mitt extended out to the side to preserve his hold on the ball, but when the glove hit the dirt, the ball dribbled out.

The umpire leaned over and dipped his masked face toward the loose ball before slashing his arms sideways through the air.

"Safe!"

The Titans spilled from the dugout, swarming Benji at the plate, but their teammate lay facedown, flat and unmoving with his arms extended. As they circled around him, the team went silent and the crowd grew quiet.

"Is he okay?" Jaden said.

Benji suddenly jerked his arms in and began pumping out sloppy push-ups over the top of home plate, counting them with a sagging bow in his back that would have embarrassed even a nerd in gym class.

After flopping out ten push-ups, Benji sprang to his feet and held his arms wide for the crowd, which erupted into earsplitting cheers. The team mauled Benji, raising him up as he grinned and bowed his head over and over.

In the tumult, Josh became aware of the heavy thud of helicopter blades. Before the Titans even settled down, the helicopter dropped from the sky and landed in a whirl of dust in the middle of the outfield. Mickey Mullen had his son by the collar, and he half guided, half dragged him toward the thundering aircraft.

As Josh and Jaden watched, Mickey Jr. escaped his dad's grip and headed toward second base. The Mick didn't even look back. He trudged for the helicopter on his own, signaling with a wave of his hand for his son to follow, but Mickey Jr. kept coming, so Josh and Jaden walked out to meet him.

To Jaden, Mickey Jr. winked and said, "Thanks for all the nice things you wrote about me. My money's on you to get that Pulitzer one day. It's been fun."

Then Mickey Jr. pointed at Josh and said, "You won this one, but next time it'll be different."

Then Mickey Jr. turned and ran for the helicopter. He hopped in, the door closed, and the helicopter rose, lifting straight up before tilting its nose and heading south.

"You did it," Jaden said, giving Josh a hug.

"And Benji," Josh said.

She nodded and said, "And Benji."

Josh looked at her, studying the golden flecks in her green eyes, looking for something—care, friendship, respect—and finding it.

"He didn't have to throw to me," Josh said, adjusting his cap to shield his eyes from the sun so he could follow the path of the helicopter as it took off into the wind. "His dad wanted him to walk me, but he threw a good pitch anyway."

"He wanted to test himself," she said, "and from what he just said, I'm guessing that he figures your paths will cross again. It's what you wanted, right? What your dad said you needed to make you great? I told you, all you had to do was be you and it would happen."

Josh looked her in the eyes and said, "I *am* looking forward to facing him again."

Still smiling, she nodded toward the helicopter growing smaller in the sky and said, "Right. It's what you said you needed to be great—a baseball rival."

TIM GREEN played Little League baseball for many years before specializing in football in order to become an NFL player. But his love for baseball lived on, inspiring him to coach his own sons' teams. After graduating as covaledictorian from Syracuse University, he was a first-round NFL draft pick and played as a star defensive end for the Atlanta Falcons. Tim also earned his law degree with honors and has worked as a commentator for FOX Sports and National Public Radio. Always an avid reader, he became the *New York Times* bestselling author of THE DARK SIDE OF THE GAME and a dozen suspense novels, including ABOVE THE LAW.

Tim has written many exciting books for young readers, including BASEBALL GREAT, also starring Josh, Jaden, and Benji; FOOTBALL GENIUS and FOOTBALL CHAMP, starring Troy White; and FOOTBALL HERO, starring Ty Lewis. FOOTBALL GENIUS and BASEBALL GREAT are both *New York Times* bestsellers.

Tim lives with his wife, Illyssa, and their five children in upstate New York. You can visit him online at www.timgreenbooks.com.